White Lies

EMILY HARPER

ISBN-13: 978-0992095307

ISBN-10: 0992095301

To my Mum and Dad, who have always encouraged me
to pursue my dreams. As George McFly once said,
"If you put your mind to it, you can accomplish anything."

This one's for you.

ACKNOWLEDGMENTS

Thank you to the many people who put so much effort and support into making me a better writer. To my beautifully talented editor, Emily Ferko, you are a master at what you do. To my writers group, who loved Natalie from the start, thank you for encouraging me to stay true to myself. And finally, to my loving husband, who drives me up the walls most days, but will always be the man of my dreams.

To The Man of My Dreams,

I know I should let fate bring us together; that we are supposed to meet one starry night on the end of a boardwalk somewhere. And don't get me wrong - that would be fab.

The trouble is this love thing is taking a *little* longer than I originally thought.

I mean, I'm a patient person, but is there any harm in trying to move things along a little? A slight push in the right direction?

So, I've decided to give fate a long needed vacation and take this matter into my own hands.

I thought you should know— in case you are also looking for me— to keep your eyes open. I'm on my way.

Hope to be seeing you soon,

Natalie Flemming.

P.S. If you're Johnny Depp, can you please just tell your assistant to put my phone calls through? It would make this whole thing a lot easier.

One

Late, as usual, I sprint to the stairwell– the elevator in the building always takes a lifetime– and start jogging up the stairs. Clutching my side on the third flight, I remember that the office is on the twenty-third floor, and at the rate I'm going the elevator might actually be the better option. Exercise is over-rated anyways.

As I wait for the elevator on the fourth floor, with the newest edition of Lasso in my arms, the possibilities reel through my head. I know I'm not pursuing love the conventional way. Trust me though, I'm looking. *Everywhere.* Putting a want ad in a magazine to find the man of your dreams is not how I envisioned meeting my Prince Charming. But, there isn't another castle besides the Royal family's near where I live, and now that William seems to be going through with the marriage my hand has been forced.

So, I have abandoned the hope of being a princess (and let's be honest, the in-laws would have been a lot of work), but I feel I have grown up and developed more realistic expectations of my future husband.

I'm an avid reader of Lasso, our company's new in-house magazine, that is supposed to be all about how to get a man and what to do to keep him; though half of the bloody thing is filled with advertisements for naughty call-in lines. It actually started out as a bit of a blip and not even our own designers wanted to read it, but they soon discovered that if you pay enough people loads of money, anything can be a success. Now, Lasso has a readership of over fifteen thousand a month (though the press package says it is twenty). Every issue, it tells us lonely hearts that men want a woman who has a mind of her own, are independent and outgoing. I read this every month, and do you know what I do? The exact opposite. I meet a man and tell him, verbatim, exactly what I think he wants to hear– which is all lies– so he'll ask me out again.

One day, while drinking a terrible cup of coffee that my co-worker Rachel made– which I always tell her is the best I have ever tasted– I flipped through the August edition. Looking at all the lovely shoes I know I would never get my feet into, let alone be able to walk in, I came across it. It was as if a light went on all around me and I could hear the 'hallelujahs' in the background. There, on page fifty-three, was the beginning of the rest of my life.

Looking for a man, but seem to be looking in all the wrong places? Wondering what is wrong with you and why you are so blue when you should be saying "I do"? Did you know that only 7% of women that meet men in a bar or club end up having a lasting relationship? No matter what your mother says, it's not you, and there is something you can do to find Mr. Right– right now! Place a want ad in next month's issue for our Month of Love special and see what fate has in store for you. Don't spend another holiday alone, hopeless, and resorting to desperate measures– resort to them now! To see your ad in the Love Wanted section just send a maximum sixty word description of your ideal mate with twenty pounds to Lasso Love Connection, 128 Foxham Street, London and see what love has in store for you.

So, I threw caution to the wind– well actually, I burned my ex-boyfriend's stuff and threw the box full of ashes into the sea, but metaphorically speaking it was kind of the same thing– and I submitted my ad.

And who knows, maybe someone famous will respond to my ad. Like some lonely, well-known actor, tired of skinny, pretentious Hollywood stars, and who just wants a normal girlfriend. Maybe Johnny Depp will respond! I've always loved him since he played that man with the knives on his hands. There is nothing sexier than a man who can chop veggies any time of the day.

The doors to the elevator open and I quickly scramble in, straightening my posture when I see a striking man leaning on the rear elevator wall, looking at his cell. Wearing a navy suit with a silver and white tie, his face is in shadows, but I can see his lips slowly moving as he reads from his phone. Turning to face the doors as they close, I look to see the floor numbers counting up before I casually glance back over my shoulder. He's still looking down. Even without the aid of styling products to keep every wavy brown hair in place he projects a casualness that seems at odds with his extremely smart attire. He has a strong jaw, and from what I can tell, a pretty good physique that he definitely didn't get from sitting behind a desk all day. My eyes focus again on the arm which is holding his phone and my breath catches. I've always loved a man's forearms and my imagination is telling me that underneath that perfectly fitted suit, his are *superb*.

He's obviously someone important, and as I look down I can't help but wish I had worn something a little more glamorous to work besides my grey pencil skirt with a thin black belt cinched around my waist.

I should have worn red: men love red dresses.

Not that I need to wear nice clothes to stand out. I mean, I'm not ugly. In fact, many people have told me I'm a natural beauty– though they usually want a favour at the time. I have blond hair (naturally brown, though I prefer to call it extremely dark blond), blue eyes with a hint of grey that sound more exciting than they actually are, and I'm a size eight, though I've found a store where a size six fits me, and now I refuse to buy my clothes from anywhere else.

As the elevator slowly rises I continue to send glances in the mystery man's direction, but he's still completely focused on his phone. I squint my eyes trying to place him. I've never seen him before; it's a large building, but I know if I'd seen him before I would remember. I try and shuffle back a little to see his face more clearly, but the two girls whispering frantically beside me block my way.

I clamp down my teeth and count to five in my head. I mean, I love gossip as much as the next girl, but don't they realize I'm trying to have a moment with this incredible sexy stranger whom I've never met? It must be really good gossip if they're not drooling all over this guy themselves. Not that they would stand a chance of course: I saw him first. Though I can't really hear what they are saying, I manage to catch "fired", "totally revamp", and "fired" again.

The elevator stops and the doors open. I wait to give a flirtatious smile to the man as he exits but it is the two other girls who get off. My nerves start to flutter when the doors close, and as the elevator rises again I can't help but pray to every God I have ever heard of for this lift to get stuck.

From under my eyelashes I glance at the gorgeous stranger, willing him with whatever internal power I possess to glance my way, but he is so focused on his phone that I'm not sure he's even blinking. I should probably leave him to it.

'Ughmm. Hmm." I cough into my hand and then place it on my chest, hoping to get his attention. He doesn't look up.

I clear my throat again and now pat my chest but he still doesn't move.

I take a deep breath and cough loudly— oh God, that sounded more like a goat— and now rub my chest.

"Are you alright?" His deep voice is even better than I could have hoped for.

I look up into the startling blue eyes of my stranger. Taken aback by his sudden attention and his interested look I almost forget to respond.

"Yes, thank you," I smile in what I hope is a self depreciating manner. "I must have had something in my throat."

His square jaw is clean shaven, though there still seems to be a shadow of stubble threatening just below the surface of his olive skin. With my hand still on my chest, the man's eyes take in its position before responding, and I can honestly say I've never been happier to be wearing a push up bra in my entire life.

"Do you work in the building?" He smiles as he asks the question, and I notice his teeth are impeccable– always a bonus.

"Yes, I work at Makka, the shoe designing firm."

His eyebrow rises ever so slightly when I say this. "What department?"

"Accounting."

He nods and puts his hand in his trouser pocket, my eyes following his every move. Realizing he is watching my gaze, I quickly dart my eyes back up to his face and add, "Accounting Manager." Detecting a hint of a smile on his face, I try not to blush.

"Do you work in this building?" I ask, trying to break the awkward moment.

He smiles again and answers, "Not yet."

"Oh, so you're looking for a job, then?" I decide right then and there if he answers yes I will fire Hank, my assistant, and mystery man is hired. Hell, I'll give him my job and I'll be *his* assistant.

"Not exactly."

"It's a tough economy out there," I say knowingly. "What field are you in?"

"Consulting, mainly," he answers. His phone starts making noises again, but this time he chooses to ignore it.

"Consulting... what exactly?" I say, trying not to sound too interested– as though I am just trying to pass the time until the elevator arrives at my floor– though, I think we both know I am intrigued by his evasive attitude.

"Oh, you know," the corner of his mouth lifts up before he answers, "this and that."

We ride the rest of the way up in silence, but I casually dart my eyes in his direction. When the lift opens at my floor I turn to say goodbye but frown when he walks to the door and holds it open, indicating me to go first.

I look at him as I pass and then stand outside, waiting for him to exit the elevator as well.

"Is this your floor?" I ask to make sure.

He nods and proceeds to open the door to Makka. I walk through, again looking at him, quickly trying to figure out what is going on.

"Are you trying to get a job here?" I can't help but sound incredulous. I don't know a single man that works here that isn't gay– except Hank, but he's just in denial.

"Not exactly." He smiles and unbuttons his jacket. The action immediately brings my attention to his abdomen, which, by the tailored fit of his shirt and trousers, I can tell he works out. A lot. If he's gay, I'm giving up on love.

"You're very mysterious." I frown and study his face for signs of what sort of game he might be playing by not telling me anything. "You're really not going to tell me what you're doing at Makka?"

He leans in and puts his lips by my ear. I can't help but take a deep breath of his cologne, and it takes all my will power not to close my eyes. "The less I tell, the more you'll wonder."

He puts slight pressure on my arm before he walks down the south corridor towards the executives' offices. Feeling surreal to the point of laughter, I look around the modern reception area to see if anyone else saw what just happened or if I somehow imagined it. Claire, our nasty receptionist, hasn't even looked up from filing her nails. Typical, no one ever sees my best moments.

Still frowning, I walk down the hall into my department and curse when I stub my toe on Rachel's desk, receiving a curious glance from Hank.

I quickly throw out "Hellos" as I sit down in my chair. When I put my bag on my desk I see my copy of Lasso poking out of the top, and with renewed determination I'm fully engrossed in the task of flipping through the magazine.

The index says wanted columns are on page thirty-four, and as I flip through I feel a surge of excitement. I mean, some man at this exact moment could be searching this magazine, read my ad, and contact me. I look at my phone and hold my breath for a few seconds, but it doesn't ring.

Okay, so the readership of Lasso is ninety-five percent females, and I'm sure the men that read it are probably gay, but still, you never know. As I scan the page I find my ad on the bottom in the left hand corner:

WANTED:

Looking for the man of my dreams, but no pressure. Seeking hard working, laid-back male. He must be an outgoing person who loves adventure, but prefers staying home at night. Tall, dark and handsome, or at least has fair features and medium height. A family man, but no children of his own. Looking for a casual relationship leading to marriage. If you are this man please write to Natalie at nflemming@lassoloveconnection.co.uk.

Oh my God, there it is. And now that I read it, it feels so surreal. Is that me? Is that my email address for anyone to write to? Suddenly, a crazy thought pops into my head– what if I get a lunatic who calls me once, likes the sound of my voice, and then won't leave me alone? What if he finds out where I live and begins to stalk me? Actually, I've always secretly wanted my own stalker.

As I close my magazine and slump in my chair, my mind is half on my ad and half on my sexy stranger. I haven't heard of any new openings at Makka, but something's going on. I see Hank and Rachel exchanging glances with each other and then back at me.

"We thought this was going to upset you," Rachel says, "but I didn't think you would get this upset so early."

"What?"

"I mean, don't feel like this is all on your shoulders," Hank continues as he puts his hand on my arm. "We'll be here to support you every step of the way."

Oh God, how did they find out?

It's embarrassing enough to have to put your bloody love life in the want ads– but to have your coworkers know, and worse, *talk* about it with you.

I should have known Hank would read Lasso.

I'll have to move away, far away. It's the only sensible solution.

Rachel sits up straight in her chair and looks at me. "They say they are bringing in outside people to see what the problem is." I can see the hope shining in Rachel's eyes. "Do you think they might need people to come in on the weekends?"

Wait a minute, they're bringing in outside help–

like a love doctor?

Oh God. That's it! That's what the elevator man is here for. He's my love doctor.

I've never had a love doctor before, but I assume he makes love to me until I fall desperately in love with him and then I'll be cured. At least I hope that's the way it works.

Hank sighs as he rearranges his vase of irises. "Frances and Michelle have already been sacked. Poor Frances was bawling his bloody eyes out when they escorted him out."

This doesn't sound right, I must have missed something. No one would get sacked because I don't have a boyfriend... right?

"What exactly did they say?" I hedge. "You know, to Frances, when they fired him."

"Oh, just you know, marketing is crap. They want a new vision, and they get the same boring ideas over and over again," Rachel shrugs as she switches on her computer and picks up the statistic reports from last month.

So, it has nothing to do with me— it's just some stupid marketing thing.

I should be relieved, but a love doctor would have been spectacular.

"Oh, and Natalie," Hank whispers while looking around to see if anyone is listening, "they mentioned your name."

"What?" My head shoots up. "What for?"

"I couldn't really understand," Hank replies, "they said something about 'pastels' and 'even the accountant noticed'."

Oh God, I thought she had forgot.

About two months ago, Nina from fabrics and I were in the loo when I heard two marketing associates chatting in the stalls– very tacky bathroom etiquette. One was telling the other that their team had a new visionary plan for Makka: pastels. Their slogan was dreadful: "You haven't been to a party until you've been to a Pastel Party."

After they'd left, Nina and I were still touching up our makeup when I snorted, "Yeah, they're so bloody visionary. Wasn't their campaign for the satin line, 'You haven't been to a party until you've worn satin on your feet'? I mean, how many parties do they go to? Besides, I wouldn't wear two hundred quid shoes to a party. Knowing my luck, someone would spill something on them."

Just as Nina broke into laughter, our senior vice president, Amelica Felix, came out of the stall and looked at me. She didn't say anything and neither did I– I was too petrified. I just picked up my bag and scrambled back to my desk as quickly as my twenty quid Primark shoes would carry me.

And Amelica remembered. I had hoped, *prayed,* she would forget, but she hadn't. Out of all the things she could have overheard, she had to hear me slagging off their ideas– their *designs.* Why couldn't she have overheard me all the times I complimented the styles? Or all the times I complained about not having a decent boyfriend?

I turn away from Rachel and Hank as they study the surrounding offices and whisper about who may get fired next.

~

I jump at any loud noises for the rest of the day. My nerves are on high alert, and I'm really not sure how much more of this I can take. Rachel and I are convinced the sexy guy from the elevator was brought in to fire people because as Rachel puts it: "The spineless gits who own the place would actually have to *do* something, which we all know is unheard of."

To pass the time I describe to Rachel, word for word, exactly what happened in the elevator. I mean, for the sake of our colleagues, and our sanity, we all need to know what is going on. Though, I might have slightly embellished mystery man and my little escapade to the point where I was pinned against the wall as he gently trailed kisses along my neck.

Afterwards Rachel and I needed to take a break to

calm down, even Hank seemed a little flushed.

Carl came by our office at lunch to ask me for my signature on a material purchase, and I practically assaulted him for any information he had.

"Crickey Natalie, I'm not really sure what the plan is." Carl peels my hands from the front of his shirt. "I do know that they are thinking about bringing in a marketing team from the outside, but besides that..." Now he is giving me a really bizarre look while glancing between my nervous twitches and the empty coffee cup on my desk.

Honestly, I haven't had that many cups. Four at the most... maybe five... and three espressos. But I have to be on high alert- none of us know who may be going next!

I convince Hank to scour the Design Department all day, trying to get any news. He actually willingly went, which I thought was very charitable of him, until I found out he was trying to get involved in the design process for the new oriental line. He came back with a sunken face when Anthony kicked him out of the department for trying on the shoes.

I also have Rachel go to the loo every half hour to see if she can score any new gossip.

I'm bloody stressed! Every five minutes someone is being escorted out in tears. The executives are meeting with everyone over the next three days to tell them how they fit into the company's "new vision".

I tell Hank and Rachel about the Amelica washroom incident, and they spend the better part of the morning reassuring me it probably means nothing that my name was mentioned. But, I can't completely rely on their opinions because I may have told them a slightly diluted version of what happened.

Actually, I told them it was Nina that made the damning comment while I simply nodded in agreement.

Luckily, the day is nearly over. I saw the executives leave about an hour ago as I hid under my desk. I didn't want them to pop their heads into our office on their way out the building to tell me I'm fired.

After the day I've had I can't wait to get back to the house and have a nice glass of sherry, but just as I grab my coat to leave the office I hear a little ping come from the computer. I quickly look around to see if anyone is near me, but the office is deserted. I look at my computer as though it is the plague and slowly inch away. Rationally, I know the executives wouldn't fire me over the internet, they would definitely tell me to my face, but I still can't stop myself from shaking. The ping rings around the office again, and I jump at the sharp noise. With another quick glance around, I press my email browser and a message pops up onto my screen.

> *To Natalie,*
> *My name is Tracey Klien, from Lasso's Love Connection.*
> *There seems to be a problem with your email, we've had a*
> *response to your ad but it keeps coming back to us.*

I have a response! Sodding technology, I always knew it would ruin my life.

> *A man named Alan Andrews is interested in meeting you.*

I got one.

To The Man of My Dreams,

I hope you have a lot of money because I may be out of a job soon.

I mean, my job is pretty crap, so I wouldn't be missing out on much... But, just in case you meet me after I've been sacked, please note I was decently employed for some time.

Consequently, if you happen to have your own business and are looking for some new talent... Or maybe I could look after your yacht or something...

Hope to be seeing you soon,

Natalie Flemming.

P.S. Obviously I would still like to meet if you don't have a yacht— a small boat would be fine as well.

Two

As I walk into Burchello's I feel a flutter of nerves. I know I promised myself that I was not going to get my hopes up about the first date that I go on, but I have secretly been imagining this all week. I mean, I might be meeting the love of my life in a few minutes.

It could be love at first sight, like that lady from Edinburgh I read about the other day. She did online dating for eight years and then ended up marrying the man next door. Okay, well, they did have to get married for him to stay in the country, and he just ran off with her savings fund, but the point is usually love is right where you would least expect it.

As I approach the maître d' I try and hide my excitement. I quickly wonder if I should ask him to make a copy of our reservations to show our children one day, but then dismiss it. I might be getting *slightly* ahead of myself– besides, I'm sure I could always pop back later for it.

I stand for a few moments politely staring at the surprisingly attractive maître d', waiting for him to address me, but he doesn't even look up. He looks familiar and I try to look closely at his face, but it's dark and nothing clicks.

"Umm… hello there," I say in a whispered tone, trying not to disturb the ambience of the lobby. "Can you tell me if my date is here yet?"

He looks up at the sound of my voice, and I have to step back from shock. Right before my eyes is my mystery elevator man.

"You!" I whisper accusingly.

"Excuse me?" He looks around to make sure that I am talking to him before closing his book and standing up straight. "Do we know each other?"

"Ha!" I can't help but laugh and look around, but no one is looking. "Of course, why would you remember me? I'm just someone who is next on the chopping block, right?"

He furrows his brow and steps a little closer, "Are you sure you have the right person?"

I shake my head at his audacity. "Oh, I'm sure. The elevator… Makka… ringing any bells?" I prompt.

A light obviously clicks on in his head, and a smile spreads across his face. "Right, the investigative journalist."

I shake my head at his joke and then poke him in the chest. "You think you were being so charming with all that 'the less you know, the more you'll wonder' business." I shake my head and cross my arms. "I'll have you know I haven't given you a second thought since I found out what a snake you are." Which is true, I hadn't thought about mystery man after I realised he was trying to sack all my friends and me.

Alright, perhaps once or twice I slipped and thought about him. But, just a little.

"What are you talking about?" He frowns and gives me a strange look, which makes me wonder if he thinks I'm crazy.

"I know they brought you in to fire all of us," I say, raising my voice and trying to be as threatening as I possibly can, which is not exactly easy when you're three inches shorter than the person you're trying to intimidate. "Let me tell you, we've all banned together. You're going to have a fight on your hands."

He grabs a hold of my shoulders and pulls me into the corner of the entryway. My breath catches as his hands effortlessly guide me away from the people waiting to be seated. He angles his face close to mine, and I can't help but smell the same cologne that made me want to swoon in the elevator. I would be lying if I said it didn't affect me, but for my colleagues— for my own self respect— I have to resist. My eyes betray my head, though, as I lower my gaze to his hard set lips, and just for a second I think about what it would be like to kiss him. The thought makes my heart beat erratically, and I quickly lift my eyes back to his slightly mocking gaze.

He lowers his voice as he says, "I'm not really sure what you are talking about, but I wasn't brought in to fire anyone. That isn't the reason I was at Makka."

"Really?" I challenge. "Then why were you there?"

He steps back slightly and somewhat reluctantly lifts his hands from my shoulders. "I'm sorry, I'm not at liberty to say. But I don't fire people, and I wasn't responsible for your friends getting sacked."

My resolve slips a bit at his words, but I try not to let it show.

Maybe I did jump to the wrong conclusion, but that still doesn't tell me what he was doing there and why he still refuses to tell me.

I open my mouth to argue some more just as a tall blond woman approaches us and drapes her hand on his shoulder.

"Oliver, there you are!" She laughs as she playfully adjusts his tie. "I thought you might have given up on me. Is our table ready?"

"I think, just about," Oliver replies as he glances over my shoulder. "Manelle, is our table ready?"

As Oliver asks this, I turn my head and see a reception desk tucked into the corner that, during my daydreaming, I must have completely missed. Manelle is a lanky man with a thin moustache in a starch white suit. The *real* maître d'.

"Oui, of course Monsieur Miles. Whenever you are ready."

I turn around and see Oliver staring straight at me, his eyes are hard, implacable, and I can't tell whether he is pleased our conversation was interrupted or not.

"I'm sorry," I hear the blond woman say in a husky voice, "Do the two of you know each other?" She looks from me to Oliver.

"No, not really," Oliver replies. "Er–"

"Natalie," I supply, "Natalie Flemming."

"Natalie," Oliver seems to test my name before continuing, "was just telling me she is here on a date. Natalie, this is my work colleague, Angelica Lewis. Angelica, this is Natalie Flemming."

"It's a pleasure, I'm sure." Angelica continues to stroke Oliver's arm while looking me up and down with a slight sneer.

With high cheekbones and a pointed chin, she is attractive in an extremely obvious way. My eyes lock with hers and I notice they're a startling violet.

I have an immediate impression that Angelica is trying to stake a claim on Oliver while letting me, not so subtly, know it.

I can't help but notice the way she clings to his arm and his apparent acceptance of it. Anyone in their right mind could see they were together, so why had he been flirting with me in the elevator? Did I make something more out of a friendly conversation than was intended? The more I study the two, however, the more I notice that Angelica is the one that is all over Oliver and not the other way around.

"Well," she smiles with a lack of sincerity, "we should get to our dinner. It was a pleasure meeting you, Natalie. I hope your date goes well tonight."

"Thank you, I'm sure it will." I move to the side as they are led into the dining room by Manelle.

Oliver never looks back, and I straighten my back and remember why I am here: to find love, or at least a decent boyfriend. I put all thoughts of Oliver and his nasty girlfriend out of my mind as I am led to my table to wait for Alan to arrive.

As I sit studying the wine list, I realize I want Alan to like me. I want this to go well. I know I shouldn't get my hopes up, I promised myself that I wasn't going to expect the first date to be the man of my dreams, but is there any harm in a little optimism? I mean, maybe he is the one... maybe he isn't...

But what if he *is* the one?

No— I mustn't think like that. I don't want to get my hopes up and then be disappointed. I want this whole experience to be a positive one, no matter what happens. "Positive thoughts, positive results," that's what Oprah always says.

As I sit, though, I wonder to myself what I would do if Alan is the man of my dreams. We might have a lovely time, get to know each other, and fall desperately in love. Paul McKenna says that if you want something to happen then you have to "see" it happen... and I definitely see Alan having a fabulous time and wondering how soon we can be married.

Okay, maybe that's too much— I see Alan having a fabulous time and wondering how soon we can be engaged.

When I look up, Manelle is pulling out the chair across from me, and Alan Andrews steps in front and sits down. I realise that of all the things that went running through my head about this date: what I would wear, what I should do with my hair, how my new signature would look when I change my last name to his— I never thought much about what *he* would look like. Which, as I think about it now, is a very odd thing to overlook.

Now that he's here, I can't believe I didn't think about it sooner. He actually looks quite... *nice*. He has a pleasant round face, with dark brown hair, and a moustache.

I wonder if he trims that himself. I've never dated anyone with a moustache before, but I like to think of myself as an equal opportunist.

His khaki jacket is fully buttoned, and as he sits down I notice the little button holes strain from being stretched. He smiles and his moustache moves with his mouth making him look like he has two sets of lips.

"You must be Natalie. I've really been looking forward to meeting you."

"And you must be Alan." I smile in return and shake his hand. "I'm sorry I wasn't able to respond to you sooner. My email is always cocking up."

"Oh, not to worry."

The waiter comes over to our table, and Alan orders some red wine. I nod in approval as I take a sip and really hope the cringe doesn't show on my face. I've always hated the taste of wine, the smell alone makes me gag. I try desperately to control the retching need to spit out the wine and finally manage to swallow it. As the waiter walks away my eyes catch Oliver's from across the room, but I quickly look away and focus all my attention on what Alan is saying, though I've missed the first bit of the story, so I end up just nodding and smiling. When the waiter returns to take our dinner order he is carrying a martini glass with him.

"A Cosmo." The waiter hands me the glass and looks uncomfortable.

"Sorry, I didn't order that," I say, pointing to the drink.

"Someone thought you would like it." The waiter subtly nods to his right. I look in the direction and meet Oliver's eyes again. Alone at his table, he lifts the corner of his mouth and raises his glass to me.

Blushing and flustered, I take the glass from the waiter and dart a glance towards Alan. He doesn't seem to notice the waiter has even returned as he carefully studies the menu. He suddenly looks up and lowers his menu.

"Oh good," he says to the waiter. "Does your prime roast come with mash?"

Throughout dinner Alan tells me all about himself. He's an only child who grew up in Lichfield. He works as a computer technician— I have to admit my mind wandered at this part of the conversation— but, he did follow up by saying he goes out to the pub on the weekend. He likes to work *and* play, he stresses.

The date carries out quite well; I explain that I work at Makka— I might have told him a story that implies I am one of the top designers, but it's not really lying if he *assumes* things, is it?

"So, Natalie," Alan reaches for his wallet, "I had a wonderful time tonight."

"Me too." I place my napkin on the table. "You know, to be honest, I didn't really expect much when I placed that ad."

"No, I know what you mean. I've been online for a while now, since my separation, but all you really get is rubbish." The waiter returns and Alan signs the Visa slip. "I've had a lovely time talking to you."

"Yes, me too." I look down at my empty martini glass and try to fight the urge to glance at Oliver's table. Throughout dinner my eyes kept betraying me, seeking him.

"We should do this again some time. Here, let me give you my business card." Alan starts rooting in his pocket while I stand up to grab my shawl.

Besides the wine, I feel this date went pretty well. I think we sort of connected with each other, and the fact he wants to do this again puts it as one of my top dating experiences. Alan finally produces the card and begins to stand up.

The more I look at his moustache, the more I begin to like it. In fact, I might add it to the criteria for my ad.

And, so he's getting divorced. At least he's been married– it shows he isn't afraid of commitment!

And, so we didn't share any of the same interests or hobbies... I'm sure I could learn to find an appreciation for bird watching. As long as they don't come near me. Or look at me. You just can't be too careful with all the disease they carry.

And, so he has a small bald spot– who doesn't? Maybe he could even shave his head like Jason Statham– that's very in right–

Wait a minute...

Is he–

I mean, is it the angle?

I think–

Is he *shorter* than me?

I take a step back, but my eyes are still over his forehead. I take another step back, but it makes no difference. And I'm not even wearing any heels!

Not that it *matters*, I mean, look at Tom and Katie... you know, before the divorce.

"Here we are." Alan hands me his card and points to the number. "My mobile is probably the best way to reach me."

"Right, fab." What is he, like five-five? I'm only four inches taller.

"You know Natalie, if you've not got anything on Saturday I'd love to take you to that restaurant I was telling you about."

"Oh, gosh. Umm..." I gaze towards the entrance, but my eyes stop just before at the table that Oliver is sitting at. "I'm not really sure what I have going on Saturday." I turn back to look at Alan, but all I can see is all my beautiful stilettos neatly lined up in my closet. "Why don't I just take your card and I can give you a call if I'm free?"

"Sure, not a problem."

We walk together to the front of the restaurant, and I try to hurry but I'm slowed down by the coat check. Once we are outside I turn to say goodnight, but I'm thrown off guard when I see Alan's face coming towards mine. I'm too stunned to move. Actually, I don't think he really thought the whole thing through as the next thing I know I'm getting a wet kiss on my chin. We both pull back and look at each other. Alan's face begins to turn bright red while I try to look anywhere else, pretending not to notice.

"Well, thanks for dinner. I better be off home." I gesture towards the taxi line up.

"Right, of course. Lovely to meet you, Natalie."

"You too, Alan." I walk to the taxi and look back. "Goodnight."

Once I am inside the taxi, I look at Alan's card and know that I won't be seeing him again.

Don't get me wrong, I think he is a lovely man. The trouble is, I'm looking for lifelong happiness and love... And I really love my shoes.

Back at the flat I feel reassured from my flatmate's reaction.

"Oh gosh– no Nat, that would never do. It seems like you guys didn't have anything in common anyways, let alone the other issue. At first I am sure it would be fine," she glances towards her bedroom where her boyfriend is snoring loudly, "but later on, when the roses have been crushed, it will just be the icing on your miserable cake."

"Wow, umm... cheers Cheryl."

Cheryl shrugs and suddenly gives a wide grin. "Though, I have heard that dating a shorter bloke does make you look thinner."

Hmm... That's a good point.

No– I have to remember my priorities. Also, I'm planning to lose a stone, so that argument is gone.

WHITE LIES

To The Man of My Dreams,

It seems our paths did not cross last night, which is slightly disappointing as I wore my good underwear– just in case.

Though, I should have known we couldn't possibly meet in a restaurant. It's too ordinary for the kind of love we'll share together. I will have to start looking somewhere more romantic, somewhere more... exotic.

Maybe I should take a trip to Fiji.

Hope to be seeing you soon,

Natalie Flemming.

P.S. Have you ever thought about growing a moustache?

Three

Perspective, that's what I need. I may have put a *little* too much hope in the first date, and I can see now that it might have been a little premature to get quotes for our Save the Date cards for the wedding. Though, it never hurts to be prepared, and in fact it helped me come to a very important decision about my future husband: he's going to have to be rich because weddings cost a bloody fortune!

I have a coffee date today with Hank and Rachel to go over our plan of action to make sure none of us get sacked. Not that we need to get our stories straight, I mean, it's not like we have anything to hide. I just want to remind them of the pinky-swear they made– that they would never tell a soul that I ruined the company's periwinkle stiletto display shoe when I tried to cram my foot into it at last year's Christmas party.

Wearing my blue polka-dot dress, I stroll through the park enjoying the beautiful spring day and lift my chin to let the breeze flow through my hair. My eyes meet the person running towards me on the jogging path, and I stop in my tracks.

"Are you following me?"

Oliver slows down to run on the spot in front of me, raising his eyebrows. "Yes, I've been jogging all over London to find you. You've saved me a lot of time though, I just finished the East side and was working my way North."

I ignore his mocking tone and concede, though only internally, that it might have been a silly accusation.

"I didn't know you lived around here. I've never seen you in this park before." I walk through this park every day, and I would remember seeing Oliver.

"I just bought a flat around the corner from here; moved in last week." He stops jogging in place and starts shaking out his legs. "Should I take your greeting as my 'welcome to the neighborhood'?"

I feel a huge gust of wind lift the bottom of my skirt as a mass of cyclists fly by us on their bikes, and I blush as I try and bring the fabric down.

"Welcome to the neighborhood," I say when everything is back in place.

"Are you on your way somewhere?" Oliver asks.

"Just to the coffee shop," I say, pointing to the building on the corner.

"Great, I could use a cup of coffee," he says and puts his hand on the small of my back to start me walking towards the shop.

My eyes go wide as I realize he plans on joining me. I can't have Oliver come inside with me; Hank and Rachel will think I betrayed them if I'm caught consorting with the enemy. Not that I'm sure Oliver is the enemy anymore, but I don't know what he is so I should still err on the side of caution.

"Oh, you can't go in there," I say, shaking my head.

"Why not?" He doesn't slow his pace.

"Because er–" I look around for inspiration but nothing pops into my head. I turn my head when I hear a baby wail and see a mummy group doing baby yoga in the park.

That is so cool. The minute I have a baby, I am definitely going to sign up–

Okay, focus Natalie.

"Because, I am going to meet my mother. And her women's group. To discuss… er… women's things," I say and hope the fear of women discussing things will be enough to deter him.

"Your mum lives nearby?" he asks.

"Yes," I nod. "Well, pretty close." Actually she lives a tube, train, and bus ride away, but I could get to her house within four hours so I feel that is close enough.

"Where does your father live?"

"I'm not sure, I never knew my father," I say and shrug.

"Oh, I'm sorry," Oliver says.

"Don't be, I don't know any different, so I've never felt like I was missing out on anything," I reason.

"So, you don't even know who he is?" he asks.

"Well, I've heard stories, but with my mother you never really know what to believe. Mum says my father was a famous poet she met when she was in Rome on an exchange in College, but my Aunty Beryl told me, after a few drinks in the pub one night, that he was a sound manager with a pop group called The Trumpets."

"You've never asked your mum about it?"

"I've never thought it was right to ask her. I grew up hearing stories of how Philippe, my father, took her to the Sistine Chapel and told her "The Creation of Adam" was like their love: two points connecting to create perfect beauty, if only for a short time. If she wants my father to be a poet rather than Philip the band manager from Slough, then what harm is that?" I ask and can't help but feel like I've maybe said too much to a man I barely know.

"Hmm." Oliver looks thoughtful but doesn't say more.

As we approach the door I smile. "Well, I'm sure

I'll see you around."

"I'll just come in and grab a cup to go," Oliver says, reaching for the door handle.

I can see Hank and Rachel sitting at a table just through the door, talking about something to each other.

"No, you can't," I argue and hastily step in front of him. "They've closed the shop to anyone who isn't a woman. They don't er– want the women's group to think they might be overheard or anything."

Oliver frowns and tries to peer through the window, but I raise my face to block his view.

"It's very secretive, to protect the innocent. You know how women are, talking about their bodies and… their… er… *feelings*," I whisper.

"Er– okay then. I'll just get a coffee up the road," he says.

"That's for the best." I plaster my body in front of the door as Charles, my neighbor from two doors down, tries to get into the shop. "They're closed to men today, Charles. Women only. You'll have to go to another one."

"What, I never heard–" he starts to argue.

"Women have rights, Charles!" I say and mentally remember to apologize to him later.

"Okay," he says, raising his arms defensively. "I'll just make a cup at home."

"Good," I say as he turns around. I shrug at Oliver, "They should really have some sort of security out here."

"Yeah," he says, nodding his head. "Well, I'll let you get to it then. You don't want to miss any of the discussion."

I nod. "See you around."

He lifts his hand in goodbye, and I watch his back until it disappears around the corner before releasing the breath I wasn't aware I was holding and enter the shop.

Crisis averted.

To The Man of My Dreams,

I strongly feel like cyclists should be banned from all parks. I mean, quite frankly, they are a danger to our society. I nearly died today.

Well, nearly died of embarrassment, but still...

Hope to be seeing you soon,

Natalie Flemming

P.S. I tried to sign up for baby yoga today and they denied me! Something to do with me needing to be a mother first, or some nonsense. I might bring it up at my next women's meeting and see if we can start a petition.

Four

Oh God, I'm late. And not just kind of late, I'm *really* late. I should have been at work an hour and a half ago.

As I run up the stairs to Makka I see Hank waiting on the steps outside the door, pacing while looking up and down the street. When he sees me he throws his hands in the air and comes running towards me.

"Thank Christ Almighty, where the bloody hell have you been?" Hank stops as I get closer and gives me a disgusted look. "And what the hell are you wearing?"

I look down at myself and the outfit does look a lot worse in daylight. I have on a jean skirt with gold buttons down the front and a cream ruffled blouse tucked into it at the waist. It's probably the black sparkly tights that are bringing the whole thing down.

"My alarm didn't go off!" I try to tug the skirt down to hide more of the tights but it doesn't budge. "Anyways, what are you doing out here? What's wrong?"

"What's wrong?" Hank grabs my arm and leads me through the entrance. "Oh, nothing much. It's just that the bosses have been looking for you for the past hour for a meeting! I told them you had nipped to the loo and I would go and get you, but that was *forty-five minutes ago.*"

"Oh bugger." I jog to the lift with Hank on my heels, and I wedge my body between the doors before they can close.

When the lift arrives at my floor I run over to the reception desk.

"Hi Claire." I'm desperately trying to catch my breath, but at the same time appear that I haven't just run a marathon to get to work. "Someone wanted to see me?"

"Yeah, like an hour ago." Claire continues typing and doesn't even look at me.

"Right, I'll just go in then, shall I?"

I walk into the boardroom and give one last tug on the hem of my skirt but it still doesn't budge. I hear a ripping noise, look down, and see one of the gold buttons from my skirt in my hand. Well, that's just perfect isn't it?

Out of the corner of my eye I see Oliver sitting at the table with his hands clasped together, and I stop in my tracks. His eyes take me in from head to toe, and now I really wish I hadn't worn this bloody skirt and legging combo today.

"Natalie Flemming." I can't help but get a fluttery feeling in my stomach from the way he says my name.

With the top button of his shirt undone, I can see the strong column of his throat under the lights. His white shirt sets off the olive colour of his skin, and even with his casual dress he looks all business. I can't help but wonder what could ruffle his feathers.

"Oh, er, hi Oliver." I look at the door and point. "I thought the executives wanted me in here, sorry."

"No, I wanted you." Sitting behind the mahogany boardroom table his presence seems to own every corner of the room. He's just too much for a Tuesday morning.

"You did?" I ask but my paranoia revs into high gear, and I become guarded. "For what?"

"Maybe you should take a seat for this." Oliver motions to the chair beside him.

"You said you don't fire people," I argue, not wanting to sit so close to those gorgeous forearms while being fired.

"That's true."

I study his face waiting for him to give something away but he doesn't blink, just pulls out the chair a fraction more.

"Because I won't go easy; I know secrets that

I'm not afraid to tell," I argue as my feet start to shuffle over to the table. "Not that I'm not extremely loyal. I've never told anyone about Carl nicking those sample shoes and selling them on eBay."

"Oh— er— okay." Oliver coughs and readjusts his chair while a smile plays with the corner of his lips. "I didn't quite hear that, so we'll just pretend..."

"Is this about the other night?" I feel the blush rising to my cheeks. "Because I've told everyone that you're not the git who's firing everyone. Not that you're a git at all," I add.

"It's not about the other night, and I'm glad that you don't think I'm a git."

"And I've made sure that rumour about you being a Russian spy was squashed," I click my tongue. "Some people let their imaginations get the best of them when they're stressed."

Actually, I do think that was one of my better theories...

"Well, that's good." Oliver looks slightly bewildered at the accusation. "I have an office in Russia, but it's too cold there. I usually send Angelica; it suits her disposition a bit better."

"Is this about my department then?" I can't help but get agitated with the subject. "I know they want to hire someone else, but really we can manage.

Rachel loves the overtime– her daughters are hideous and she can't stand going home–"

Oliver covers my mouth with his fingertips, and the action causes my voice to stop working. The amusement in his eyes makes my knees go weak and my heart to skip a beat. He leans forward, and the heat from his body sends a warm glow over my skin.

"It might be easier if I just tell you why I wanted you."

My head bobs and I murmur "okay" against his fingers.

The vibration from my lips on his hand causes his gaze to focus on my mouth, and he gently runs his finger over it before he withdraws his hand.

Frowning, Oliver looks at his fingers as though he is unsure why he did that. *I'm* not sure why he did it, but I'm also definitely not complaining.

Sitting back in his chair, Oliver visibly withdraws as he readjusts the already tidy papers in front of him before lifting his gaze.

"Natalie, I actually called you in here to talk about the new marketing campaign for Makka."

"The new marketing campaign?" I frown and can't help but feel slightly foolish. "That's what you're here for?"

Oliver dramatically sighs as his eyes sparkle with mischief. "See, isn't the fun of the wonder so much better than reality?" He looks thoughtful as he adds, "Though being a Russian spy would be very interesting."

Alright, perhaps I did get a little carried away.

"My company, Westcott Solutions, has been outsourced to oversee the new marketing campaign, as well as the rebuild of the Marketing Department itself," Oliver explains.

"Oh– er– okay." I take out the small pen and mini note pad I keep tucked into my bra strap. "Did you want to go over a budget?"

"Did you–" Oliver clears his throat. "Do you always keep that there?"

"What? Oh this?" I shrug holding the pen and notepad in my palm. "Always be prepared, it's the Girl Guide motto."

"You were a Girl Guide?" Oliver looks skeptical as he takes in my long legs and stilettos.

"Well, no, not *exactly*. I wanted to date the Boy Scout leader in grade school so I did a little research, and I thought some of their arguments were quite valid."

I lick my finger and turn the notepad to a fresh page, only to look up again and see Oliver's astonished face.

"You're going to be trouble– I know it." He seems to say this to himself but loud enough that I catch it.

"So, umm..."

"I wanted to discuss the marketing campaign and your involvement in it." Oliver sits forward in the chair.

"Right, well I run a tight ship in Accounting. No slacking off. Though, we do break for tea at one– Hank's unbearable if he doesn't eat–"

"Actually," he interrupts, "I didn't want to discuss accounting. I wanted to discuss marketing."

"Well, I'm not sure what help I can be. We do have a Marketing Department here." A really crappy one, but I choose not to mention this.

"It says here you expressed some interest in marketing at a team building exercise a few years ago." I look down at the yellow folder in his hand and my suspicions peak.

"Is that my file?" I say in outrage. "They wrote that in my *file*?" How the bloody hell did he get his hands on my file? I know they are locked up somewhere safe because I once had a go trying to steal Claire's. I wanted to put some incriminating evidence in it when she "accidently" let her dog go to the bathroom in my office.

"You graduated with a degree in finance and marketing so you were qualified to apply."

"What else is in my file, what does it say?" I

demand and lean forward, but Oliver closes the folder. Oh God, I hope they didn't put in that time my shirt was open for an entire board meeting and no one told me my bright pink bra was showing.

"I'm sorry, it's confidential," Oliver says in mock seriousness, which just irritates me further.

"It's *my* confidentiality– I want to see it," I argue.

"Are you interested in working for marketing?" Oliver asks, and I can't help but feel he is trying to distract me.

He obviously doesn't know me very well.

"Why were you looking in my file?" I suspiciously ask.

I see his composure slip a little at the question, but his cool mask is quickly replaced, and he casually answers, "I've been going through all the files, looking for potential."

"Really?" I ask skeptically. "You went through all hundred-something employee files?"

We stare at each other, challenging the other not to flinch first, he finally shrugs. "Most of them."

Call it women's intuition, but I don't think he looked through anyone else's.

My fingers are itching to get onto that file, and it takes everything within me not to grab it from Oliver's hands.

I'm not sure I would even want to see it if he

wasn't being so stubborn about it. Alright, that's a lie. I *need* to see it.

"You know, you're right. I don't need to see that file." I say, lifting my gaze to the wall behind Oliver's head. "Oh, umm, what's that?"

It's not ideal, but it's my only chance. I leap forwards in my chair, perhaps a little more forcefully than necessary, and plow into Oliver's chest. Oliver takes the brunt of the fall, the weight of our two bodies causing the chair to fall backwards, and his shoulders slam against the ground. I'm not exactly sure what I had hoped to achieve with this move.

His arms are firmly wrapped around me, blocking me from the impact, and I lay on top of him with my head pressed against his solid chest in shock. I can hear his heart beat and although it's fast, it is nowhere near the racing pace of mine.

"Natalie, are you alright?"

"Er– yes, yes I'm fine." Just extremely embarrassed. "I thought– umm– I tripped."

"Sitting down?" I can feel his body relax as the chuckle vibrates Oliver's chest; the feeling of his warm body and male scent is intoxicating.

Through his shirt his chest feels hard, but his embrace is all encompassing and I can't help but close my eyes at the feeling. Oliver's chin rests on my hair, and I hear his gentle intake of breath.

Oh my God, I think he is smelling my hair. Maybe we should lie here for a minute or two, just to make sure nothing's broken.

I hear the door click open and Hank's voice, "Sorry to interrupt, I oh-" I turn my head to see Hank's shocked expression as he raises his hands. "Oh God, sorry, I didn't mean to disturb." He slowly backs up and I scramble from Oliver's embrace.

Oliver pushes on my forearms to help me from the awkward position. When I'm finally standing my hair is everywhere and my skirt has ripped further up my thigh.

"It's not what it looks like," I argue. "I tripped and-"

"Oh, you don't have to explain anything to me, Natalie." Hank winks and grins as he walks out of the room and closes the door.

Great, within the hour everyone will be thinking we had sex in the boardroom.

I tug on my skirt and shake my head. Why did I think that would work?

My eyes search for the file, but it's back in Oliver's hands. He's also managed to straighten the chairs already.

I can still feel the warmth from his chest on my face, and I notice Oliver's slightly rumpled shirt. On the outside he seems composed, but the tenseness of his jaw reminds me that he wasn't as immune to the embrace as he looks. I could use this to my advantage.

"Oliver, are you sure you're alright?" I take my seat again while attempting to smooth my hair into some semblance of order. "Do you need to take a minute, perhaps step out of the room for a glass of water?"

Oliver shakes his head and I can tell he's on to me. In fact, I am starting to think he knows I didn't trip. Imagine!

"It's probably better if I don't leave you alone. You never know if there will be a stray rock or a loose floorboard."

Alright, he definitely knows.

"So, Natalie about your marketing ambitions—"

"Listen, I'm not sure what that file says," mainly because he won't show me the bloody thing, "but whatever it says it's not true. I'm happy where I am now."

Okay, that's not entirely true. I actually hate accounting, and, to be quite honest, I'm not sure that I'm very good at it. I am always shocked at the end of tax season when the HM Revenue and Customs doesn't show up and say I've cocked the whole thing up.

But, I'm definitely *not* interested in marketing. After what happened last time…

"It was all just a misunderstanding." I try and laugh but it comes out more like a strangled cry.

Oliver opens the file folder before meeting my gaze. "So you didn't say that marketing was run by a 'Narcissistic Bastard', and you wouldn't give Makka another one of your brilliant ideas if your life depended on it?"

Wow, they really have everything in that file.

"Well, if you say it like that it sounds bad, doesn't it? But, if you knew the whole story…"

"Tell me, then." He closes the file and leans back in his chair.

I forget my need to look at the folder as I see the genuine interest on Oliver's face.

"It was just a crazy misunderstanding." I try and laugh but it sounds half-hearted, even to me.

"I was hired here as a junior accountant, though I was always more interested in marketing at school. I was dating the marketing coordinator here because he was charming and I thought he was a nice enough guy, not because I wanted a promotion," I amend. "But, after a few months I tried to hint to him that I was interested in marketing, just to feel him out. I even told him some of my ideas."

I take a deep breath and look at my sweaty palms

resting in my lap. "At the team building meeting when I called him... well you know what I called him... the meeting quickly turned nasty and each department was having a go at each other, but marketing was taking a particularly bad beating. Everyone was complaining that the slogans and advertisements were crap. The narcissistic bast– er– Spencer, got really defensive and started blurting out some new ideas. All of *my* ideas."

I can feel my face go flush from anger even though it happened years ago. I know I should let it go and move on– and I thought I had– but I guess forgetting and forcing yourself not to remember aren't exactly the same thing.

"I wouldn't have minded, only I'd asked him for a job the night before. I knew marketing was struggling a bit," I explain.

"And he turned you down," Oliver guesses. "You were more than qualified, so why would he do that?"

"I don't know,' I shrug.

"Maybe he didn't want people to think he was giving you any special treatment, so he was going to see how the team reacted and then give you the credit," he suggests.

"No, he was never going to give me the credit," I argue.

"Did he say that to you?"

"When he said those ideas— my ideas— something inside me snapped and I stood up and told him those were my ideas, and if he thought that they were so brilliant then why wouldn't he give me a job?"

"And?" Oliver prompts.

"And he said that I might have had one or two good ideas, but I wasn't a creative enough person to come up with any more."

"He said—" Oliver seems to change his mind. "Is there more?"

"Nothing worth mentioning." Oh God, I really hope he changes the subject now and drops this whole thing.

"Did he explain why he didn't think you were creative?"

I furrow my brow in what I hope looks like concentration. "Er— no— I mean, I don't think so..."

Oliver's eyes seem to challenge me as he leans forward. "Natalie, I can't help you if I don't know the whole story."

"Who said I wanted any help?" I blurt out. "I don't want to work in marketing. I'm happy where I am so what does it matter?"

"Because you're selling yourself short if this is what you're passionate about, and I'm not going to sit here and let you because you're afraid–"

"I'm not afraid!" I defend myself.

"Then why won't you tell me?" Oliver presses. All of the earlier laughter is erased from his face, and the seriousness etched into every line makes me want to squirm. It also makes me want to tell him.

Oh, sod it.

"Fine! You want to know what he said?" I yell and stand up with my hands braced on the table. "He said he knew I wasn't a creative person from the way I was in the bedroom. Happy now?"

I collapse into my chair and feel the burning in my chest forcing tears into my eyes, and I have to fight to breathe steadily. I don't want to cry about this again, it's not worth my tears.

I don't want to look at Oliver. I *can't* look at him. I hate the sympathy in people's eyes when I tell them the story. If anything, it makes the whole thing even worse.

"It is what it is." I shrug my shoulders.

When I got back to the office after Spencer's little revelation, I had a quick look through Hank's Karma Sutra, and there is no way I could do those positions and realistically fake it.

I try to meet Oliver's eyes, but the look on his face startles me. The professional, composed Oliver is gone.

"He *said* that to you?" His words are clipped, and all I can do is nod my head.

"That–" Oliver's jaw tenses causing a vein to throb at the side of his head. "And you believed him?"

"I–" I frown and shake my head. "I guess so."

To be honest, I had never really thought I had an option *not* to believe him before.

"Natalie," Oliver seems to be choosing his words carefully, "I've known you for less than a week, and I can honestly say you are one of the brightest, most innovative people I know."

"It happened five years ago Oliver, and really, I'm fine. It turned out better this way."

Especially for Malcolm who got the marketing position, and eventually took over for Spencer when he left.

"Be a part of the new marketing campaign." He doesn't mince words, this guy.

"Oliver, no, I can't. I have an Accounting Department to run."

"Then you can join as a consultant until the Gala, and see if it's something that interests you. Malcolm's contract is up the week after the unveiling, and he has hinted that he is putting his CV out to other companies."

"I don't think it's a good idea–"

"Try for one day," he compromises. "If you don't like it, then I'll forget about the whole thing."

From his determined look I doubt this very much. Oliver doesn't seem like the type of man who would concede easily, though I'd be lying if I said my resolution wasn't wavering just a little.

"What would I have to do exactly?" I hedge.

"We'll start small," Oliver assures me. "You can give me a tour tomorrow to assess the situation."

"Tomorrow?" He wants to start that soon? "I'm not sure if this is a good idea..."

"If you agree," he leans forward and scans the room, though he knows no one is there, "I'll let you see the file."

My eyes widen and I lick my lips as I look at the folder filled with papers.

"Remind me again what I would have to do."

To The Man of My Dreams,

I am being forced to do something against my will, so now would be an excellent time to come riding in on that white horse of yours and draw your sword.

Not that I need you to fight my battles or anything. I mean, I'm an independent woman.

Though, if you should happen to feel it necessary to fight my battles for me on this *particular* occasion, then I feel I am an independent enough woman to let you do that.

Hope to be seeing you soon,

Natalie Flemming.

P.S. I should probably mention that Makka has a strict policy against weapons in the workplace, so you can just bring a plastic sword for show (I'm sure no one will notice the difference anyways).

Five

I have been cheated. The file had a few pieces of worthless information about me and some of my performance reviews (which I had to sign– so it wasn't anything new). The rest were blank pieces of paper, which Oliver obviously put in there to make it look more enticing. It also only briefly mentioned the meeting with Spencer, saying I had shown interest in marketing with a red pen mark at the bottom which said: *Accused Marketing Director of being a narcissistic bastard. Follow up?*

They hadn't even indicated whose side they were on, which is slightly disappointing.

Anyways, the point is, he tricked me.

Well, two can play this game. I'll give the tour of a lifetime today, being really positive about everything. I'll show him how brilliant I am, and then when he asks me to be a part of the marketing campaign, I will turn him down flat.

Yes, that will show him who's boss.

I have decided to take the afternoon today to re-evaluate my situation. I made Hank and Rachel help me get through all our work early. Now, Rachel is sewing her daughter's ballet costume for her recital next week, while Hank is looking through the paper for Cher concert tickets.

I need to figure out where I am going wrong to see how I can make things right. Even Socrates said, "An unexamined life is not worth living." And he seemed to be pretty successful, I mean, he had his own book and everything, didn't he?

I've decided to make a list of areas that require... *attention*.

1. Love life.
2. Job has gotten worse, due to an unwanted intervention.
3. I've either gained weight or shrunk my jeans again. Neither option is very good.
4. Spent rent money on that exercise machine off the telly.
5. Need to figure out how to put exercise machine together.

Actually, after re-evaluating my situation I don't feel any better. In fact, all it did was remind me how disappointing it all is. My life is not in the exact location I was hoping it was going to be at this point.

I pop into the loo before I go back to my office after my lunch break. As I walk back to my office while fighting an unruly curl that won't stay behind my ear, I look up to see Oliver leaning against my office door, lazily watching me. The second he sees me looking, he seems to come out of some sort of trance and a serious, more professional look, takes over his features.

"Ready for my tour?" he asks as he pushes himself off the wall and comes to stand beside me.

"Of course," I say, trying to sound as professional as possible.

"Lead the way," he lifts his arm to indicate for me to go first, and I lift my chin and stride past him.

He looks annoyingly relaxed to me and I quickly go over in my head the tour that I have planned for him. The office isn't very big, consisting only of four main departments, so I figure I could get this whole thing over and done within ten minutes if I stick to the plan.

Alright, I'll admit the thought of being a part of the marketing campaign is extremely exciting, but that doesn't mean it's the right thing to do. I got burned very badly last time I tried something new and exciting (and I'm not talking about the At Home Hot Stone Massage Kit I bought– though I still have a mark on my bum from it). No, for once I'm going to be sensible.

"I think we should probably just start at the beginning." I lead him to the entrance of Makka.

"This is our reception area with our... er... lovely receptionist, Claire." Claire doesn't even look up from her desk.

"She's umm... a bit preoccupied I guess." I start walking and Oliver continues beside me. "And this is the Accounting Department, which I am responsible for."

I came in early this morning and tried to make our office as colourful and exciting as possible. Though, I'll admit, trying to make accounting exciting is not the easiest thing to do. As we enter my office Hank is leaning over Rachel's shoulder reading an article.

"Nat, you have to come and read this." Hank is still engrossed in the article and doesn't notice that I am not alone. "A lady from Sussex has just married her Pomeranian."

I blush and don't dare look at Oliver. "Hank, Rachel, this is Oliver Miles," Hank and Rachel look up, "the new Marketing Consultant."

Hank falls backwards into the filing cabinet to avoid Rachel who has jumped out of her seat and raced over to Oliver.

"Mr. Miles, of course. Rachel Wedford– junior accountant here at Makka. So pleased to meet you." Rachel vigorously shakes Oliver's hand. "Let me be the first to say I am all for change, no matter the hard work or long hours. In fact, if you ever need anyone to stay behind, work weekends..."

Hank rolls his eyes behind Rachel and runs his hands over his leather pants before stepping in front of her.

"Hank Clive, Mr. Miles– the *other* junior accountant." Hank leans in towards Oliver and lowers his voice. "Bloody mess they've made here. You know if you ever need any help in marketing, I did do quite a bit at my last job."

"Right," Oliver says and takes out his notepad, "and where was that at?"

"Marks and Spencers, Lingerie Department. I use to pick which knickers went on the mannequins."

Perfect.

"Hank is a genius," I say, walking over until I'm standing next to him. "In fact he has a whole design book of great ideas." Hank's face beams at my compliment, and I can't help but feel a little guilty using Hank like this. I've seen his book more than once and to be honest it's nothing to write home about.

"That's great, Hank. You know I'm all for people stepping out of their comfort zones," Oliver pats Hank on the back, and I can tell Hank is enamoured with Oliver's charming smile. "If you have a gift for something you shouldn't let anything hold you back."

Oliver shoots me a glance from the corner of his eye, obviously looking to see if I got his subtle message.

Right, well that one back fired, didn't it?

I step towards the door and indicate for Oliver to pass. I look back into my office to shake my head, but Hank and Rachel are already excitedly whispering to one another.

"I think we should go to Fabrication next." We turn left down the hallway. "Most of the stuff we ship to China– er– another company to manufacture, but the finishing touches we do all in house."

I open the door to Fabrication to see piles of feathers everywhere. Carl is directing people to stand in a straight line with piles of feathers in their arms while he goes up and down plucking them from different people.

"Oh excellent," I smile eagerly, "we must have come at a crucial time."

"Natalie! What are you doing here?" Carl approaches and kisses me on both cheeks. "The last time you walked through those doors I had to cut your hair after you got it tangled in your bra strap, remember?" Carl laughs while I feel the blush rising all over my body.

"Not really," I mumble and don't dare look at

Oliver. "Carl, this is Oliver Miles, the new Marketing Consultant. I'm just showing him the different departments."

"Perfect, then you both can help me." Carl walks back to his models.

"You don't mind, do you?" I say to Oliver. "This type of thing happens quite often here. People seem to seek out my opinion— probably because I can be objective." I shrug like it's no big deal, while Oliver takes a seat at the large design table looking happy to see what unfolds.

This is perfect, I can show Oliver that I express my creative side every day. If he sees that I am sought after even though I am the accountant, he might feel satisfied that I am happy where I am and leave me alone.

This will definitely work.

"Now, I must know what you both think." Carl comes back and has three feathers in his hand.

I touch each one very thoroughly with my finger tips. Then for some reason I take each one to my face and sniff it. I have no idea what I am looking for, though I must be doing something right as Carl keeps nodding and encouraging me. Oliver is watching with that same amused smile on his face.

"Now, I love the rich texture of the first one," I say, holding it up.

"Right, yes, that's what I was thinking." Carl nods.

"But then I love the... er... soft subtle lines of this one." I point to another.

"At a standstill, just like me." Carl throws his arms in the air and sits on the stool.

"Well, perhaps if I see the shoe, I might have a better idea," I say.

"Shoe?" Carl asks while picking up another feather. "What shoe?"

"The shoe the feather is for."

"Oh, it's not for a shoe." Carl waves his hand. "I'm trying to decide what feather pillow to put in my new bedroom. You know I had Laurence Llewelyn-Bowen design the whole room."

Oh for God's sake.

I don't even bother saying anything to Oliver as I lead him out of Fabrication and into Design.

"And this is our Design Department," I say as we round the corner. "This is where the magic happens."

I dramatically open the door and smile, but the smile is quickly erased from my face. Anthony and Sarah are sitting on the design table playing scissors, paper, stone; the rest of the department is deserted.

"Right, well, they must be on lunch."

Oliver looks at his watch and raises his

eyebrows.

Well, people have been known to take their lunches a little late here. I mean, it can't be later than one o'clock.

I look down at my watch.

Wow– it's three-fifteen already. Yes, well, I do suppose this looks *slightly* bad.

"But you should see them in action," I pick up a pair of the design shears from the shelf, "it's like they're magic wands!" As I wave them in the air to demonstrate one of the handles falls off.

"Right," I say, trying to put them down without drawing attention to the handle that is on the floor, "I think I should show you Marketing next."

Oliver opens the door for me to pass through and follows as I walk down the corridor.

Things aren't really going the way I'd planned them. I was going to show him the company at its best, be positive about everything, show him how brilliant I am and then turn him down when he asked me to be a part of the marketing team, because there wasn't meant to be anything to fix. I wanted to show him how happy I am with the company, how lovely my job is, but it all looks terrible. Everyone has either buggered off for the day or is planning their latest bedroom remodel.

"And this is the Marketing Department." I lead

Oliver through the doors and stop dead in my tracks.

Oh God, it's worse than Design. Fortunately there are more people in here, but they all look so *depressed*. One person is sitting in the corner shaking their head at the blank computer screen, while the person sitting behind them has their head down on their desk crying. The rest just look like zombies; reading and typing things with a haunted look on their faces with their hair sticking out.

"Right, well..." I run my hand through my hair. "Usually, it's a bit more–" The crying woman has let out a wail and the rest of the department hasn't even noticed.

"Oh, what's the point?" I throw my arms in the air. "You can see them; you can see what it's like. It's bloody miserable. They've been coming out with the same dribble for the past decade and the executives told them it was fantastic. The execs changed their minds because naff all was being sold and now this lot wouldn't know a good idea if it bit them on their Gucci-clad arse."

I collapse into the nearest chair and put my head in my hands.

"Natalie?" Oliver bends down on one knee in front of me and puts his hand on my shoulder to get my attention. When I look up he is smiling. "I think that's the first truthful thing you've said all afternoon."

"Well, there isn't much to work with, is there?"
I gesture around the room.

Oliver nods and looks at all the zoned out faces.
"Well, from a marketing standpoint, I find it's always
best to start with the truth and to... *expand* from
there."

I look into his eyes and I can see them smiling
back at me. He looks so lovely when he's relaxed like
this. I think if he asked me to be a part of the
marketing team right this moment, I wouldn't have
the willpower to say no. Another wail from across
the room reminds me we are in a crowded office, and
Oliver removes his hand from my arm and stands up,
buttoning his jacket.

"Well, I think I know where we stand now." He
looks around the room.

"You do?" I ask, my eyes never leaving his face.

He lowers his eyes at the double meaning to my
words, but obviously chooses to ignore it. "So, what
do you think? Will you be a part of the campaign?"

"Oliver, I'm not sure this is a good idea. I
haven't done any sort of marketing for over seven
years," I venture as I stand up and take in our
surroundings.

"You may be right. It might not work out,"
Oliver admits but then gives me a dazzling smile that

makes my knees a little weak. "But we'll never know unless you try."

"Well here's your office, then." I shove a pile of boxes away from the door. "It's a bit cramped, but at least you have a window."

When I point to the window, I wish I hadn't. It's covered in dirt and you can barely make out the advertisement for male underwear on the building next door.

"Oh, Olly and I are used to cramped, dark places," I hear from the doorway.

I turn around to see Angelica walk past me and drape her arm on Oliver's shoulder.

Damn, I forgot about her.

"I'm sure we will manage somehow," she purrs. "But what we're going to do with this company might be a little more challenging."

I bristle at her comment and straighten to stand taller. I mean, I'm the first to get in line for slagging this place off to colleagues, but if she thinks I am going to stand here–

"I mean in situations like this you really have to wonder if it's worth it." Angelica places her briefcase on the desk and starts bringing out files. "Of course, you can make it work, Olly; you're a genius at this. But do they have any *talent* to sustain it themselves?"

Right, this cow is going down.

I open my mouth to tell her what *her* talents consist of, but Oliver beats me to it.

"I don't believe we should ever give up on clients, Angelica. They may be a little worse for wear right now, but they've been at the top before." Oliver moves the files Angelica placed on his desk to the side and places his own briefcase in their place. "Sometimes we all need to be reminded how we got to where we are."

If I didn't know better I would say Angelica looks affronted at Oliver's rebuke, but then she laughs and picks up her files. "Of course, you know what you're doing, Oliver," she puts her finger on his chin, "that's why you're the boss."

Oliver narrows his eyes in warning before stepping back, but she ignores the look and I can't help but frown at the exchange.

"Hopefully it won't take longer than projected. We're due in Germany in two months." Angelica walks past me. "I'll be next door if you need me."

Oliver walks back over to the window to gaze out— though I am pretty sure he isn't looking at anything in particular as you can't make much out through the dirt.

"Well," I laugh, "she's encouraging."

"Yes," Oliver smiles and turns his head to look

at me. "Angelica doesn't have a lot of patience." He pulls back the desk chair and removes his jacket. I watch him take it off, revealing his wide shoulders, and my mind starts to slowly undress the rest of him. I have to blink rapidly to remember what we were talking about.

"Well, that's an excellent quality to have in your business," I joke with a slight catch in my breath. "Why on earth don't you fire her, then?"

After the words come out I can't believe I have said them. This is what happens when a man takes off his jacket in front of me, well at least when Oliver does. Obviously he wouldn't fire her if they're... involved.

"What Angelica lacks in social skills, she makes up for in talent." Oliver pauses to look at the wall to the office next door. "She's very good at what she does and it makes more sense to have her working for me than against me."

I nod. "Yes, she can be... intimidating, I guess." A complete and utter bitch is probably a better way of putting it.

Oliver looks at my scowl and then laughs. "I'm sure you could hold your own with Angelica Lewis."

I shake my head in denial. "I've never been good with confrontation. It's something I avoid at all costs."

"Sometimes avoiding confrontation is actually the brave thing to do," Oliver idly comments.

"Well, I wouldn't call it brave." I laugh while thinking of all the people that I've let intimidate me. The executives, Spencer, Angelica. And that's just at work.

Oliver lifts a box from the floor and my breath catches as his strong arms flex under his shirt sleeve. Suddenly a picture of Oliver lifting me into his arms flashes through my mind, and I shake my head to get back to reality. "Well, I better leave you to crack on with it then."

I slowly start to walk to the door.

"Natalie?" I stop and turn around to look at Oliver, who has followed me.

"Yes?"

"I like your hair down like that. It looks pretty."

"I– thank you." I say as my fingers reach for the curls.

"Did you enjoy the tour today?"

"Yes, thank you." I stay frozen in place not sure what else to say.

"This marketing campaign, hell, this Marketing Department would benefit from your involvement." Oliver nods his head with certainty. "I think you would benefit, too."

I spent the day trying to convince Oliver I was

happy in my job, but I wonder if I was trying to convince myself as well. I have a good job, a job I should be happy with, but I would be lying if I said I was.

I loved marketing in school, and I was good at it too. Maybe it wouldn't be such a bad thing to try it out again. I could contribute to the marketing campaign and see if I like it. If nothing else, it might help me let go of the past.

"Okay." I nod my head in agreement to myself as much as Oliver.

"Okay?" he asks to be sure.

"I'll help with the new campaign."

A smile of victory spreads across Oliver's face.

I play with the hem of my skirt as I try and work up a bit of courage. "Maybe, umm– Maybe we should talk about the whole campaign over dinner?"

I know I should have waited for him to ask me out, but playing hard to get has never been my strong suit.

"Actually, that sounds perfect." Oliver walks behind his desk and picks up his journal.

I can barely stop myself from jumping up and down and squealing. Though, I'm not ashamed to say it's the first thing I will do when I get back to my office. "I'll have to see when everyone else is free though," he says as he flips to the next page.

Wait, what?

"Everyone else?" I say without trying to sound deflated.

"Angelica and I have dinner plans today and tomorrow. Maybe the day after that?" He looks to me for approval.

"Angelica will be there?" I know for self-preservation purposes I should try and hide the disappointment in my voice but the effort is half-hearted and it obviously shows from Oliver's puzzled look.

"Yes, well, she *is* helping with the new campaign," he says and lowers his journal.

"Right," I say tight-lipped. God, I feel like such an idiot. Why do I always make something more out of what's really there?

Oliver's eyes narrow. "Is something wrong?"

"Wrong?" I shrug my shoulders. "Nothing's wrong."

Oliver comes round his desk to stand in front of me again. A suspicion seems to be growing in his head.

"Unless you would like to talk about it with me first? Go out to dinner just the two of us?"

Great, that's all my pride needs– a pity date.

"No, it makes sense to have everyone there." I purse my lips. "Though it might be hard to pin everyone down. You and Angelica have a date tonight, so today's not good." I cross my arms and put my finger to my mouth thinking.

"It's actually a *business* dinner-"

"I have a date tomorrow night," I lie. "But the night after that might work."

"You have a date?" Oliver narrows his eyes. "With the wine guy?"

"No." Honestly, the way he says "wine guy". Alan was a lovely man, except for the height issue, and the baldness and the fact he had the ability to bore me to tears... "Someone else."

Oliver stays quiet and I'm not sure if I'm supposed to say something, or if he is.

"Fine," he puts both hands in his pockets, "Friday then."

"Fine," I answer.

Standing there, staring at the wall, I feel like a complete prat. I'm not sure why I'm so upset, I mean, I was the one who asked him to dinner. But, I just don't understand him. One minute he's flirting with me and the next minute he's all business.

"Well, I should get back at it." I point to the door and slowly back up.

He nods and sits down at his desk, watching me as I slowly retreat. When I finally get to the door I give a final nod in his direction and scurry back to my desk.

Well, that went well.

To The Man of My Dreams,

I've made a complete and utter fool of myself in front of my boss. Well, he's not actually my boss– at least, I don't think he is. But I'll be seeing a lot of him in the near future and I think I have successfully kicked the awkward level up to red alert.

Why do I always build things up in my head that are clearly not there? Maybe I should consult a doctor. It could be some rare disease that only women get that I haven't heard of.

Hope to be seeing you soon,

Natalie Flemming.

P.S. Please don't feel insanely jealous or that you need to come in and kiss me passionately in front of my entire workplace in order to claim me as your own. Though, if you feel it is the only way...

Six

Right, I'm not going to let the thing with Oliver get me down. I shaved my legs today and by God I am not going to waste them sitting at home.

I received James's response to my ad yesterday before the disastrous tour. I was going to tell him I wasn't interested, but after... well... you know what happened. He said to meet him at a bar not too far from work, so I leave straight from the office to meet him.

I did a quick wardrobe change in the loos, but decided that it was probably going to be more of a casual date than anything, so I went for a more natural look with my hair and makeup.

When I enter the bar, I search the room for a lonely face that could belong to James. I should have gotten him to wear a carnation so I would be able to recognise him. All the faces are interacting with another person, so I head to the bar to wait it out there.

I take a seat on one of the high-rise stools and wait for the barman to notice me. As the barman turns I can't help but feel a flutter in my stomach. He is gorgeous– and that may be an understatement.

He has wavy hair that my mother would say needs a good cut,   and eyes that are a piercing grey outlined with dark eyelashes– the kind a woman will buy a million products to try and replicate.

But that's one of the sad truths of the world– men have the best calves and eyelashes.

He's wearing form fitting jeans with a tight black t-shirt, which leaves nothing to the imagination, but makes my mouth water.

Even though I am here to meet James I can't help but give a sheepish grin and blush when the barman comes over and asks me what I would like to drink.

"A martini, please."

He places a napkin down in front of me and an empty glass. When he begins to pour I notice his strong arms flexing under his t-shirt and it takes all my concentration not to swoon.

"Meeting someone here?" He asks as he places some pretzels in front of me in a little bowl.

"Yes, but I don't think he's here yet." My voice comes out in a bit of a whispery tone as I play with the small straw.

"Well, what's his name?" The barman replaces the bottle of liquor under the counter. "I know a lot of people who come in here; I might be able to point him out for you."

"Oh," I toss my hair over my shoulder and look around the room again, "a man named James."

The bartender gives a wide grin and leans forward. "As a matter of fact, I do know him."

"Great," I sit up straighter on my stool and frown when I look around the room again. "Is he here yet?"

"He sure is."

"Well," I peer over the heads of the people sitting around me, "where is he?"

"You're looking at him." The barman steps back and puts his hands on his hips.

I look at the barman and frown in confusion until the light clicks on in my head.

"*You're* James?" I ask incredulously.

Now, I don't like to be self depreciating and all— but if this guy has to search the want ads to find love then I might as well join the convent now. I wonder if the celibacy thing is optional...

"You must be Natalie." He extends his hand.

"I am." I feel light headed as I reach over the bar to shake his hand. "When you said you work close by, I didn't think this actually was your work. Why didn't you tell me you work here?" I laugh self consciously.

"Yeah, well my shift is just ending so I thought it best to just meet here. I like to vet out my possible dates, so if I don't like what I see when they come in, I just tell them James called and said he couldn't make it." He puts the rag he wiped the counter with under the bar and gestures over his shoulder. "Let me just go and tell Mark that I'm off and we can leave."

I watch him go and talk to the other barman and still cannot believe my luck. I have never dated a guy like this before. And I made it past his first test! Alright, so his test is pretty chauvinistic, but my vanity is still pretty pleased.

James disappears through the doorway at the back, and then in no time at all is by my side to lead me out of the bar.

"So, what are we going to do tonight?" I ask.

"Well, I thought maybe we could try rock climbing."

"*Rock climbing?*"

"Unless you're not up for it," James says as he leads me down a street.

"No— rock climbing— absolutely. I mean it's been a while..." I shrug, "but it's like riding a bike, isn't it?"

God I hope not, I didn't take my training wheels off until I was nine and a half— even then I only did it for show.

"So, you've rock climbed before, then?"

"Oh definitely," I nod, "I just climbed Stinchcombe last year."

"Right," James frowns, "I've never heard of that rock formation, is it in England?"

I nod.

Alright, well it's not exactly a *rock formation*. It's more like a big hill near Mum's house we had to climb with her women's group to raise money for some charity last year. Though, I was out of breath by the time I finished, so it was just as challenging as climbing a rock, I'm sure.

"So how long did it take you, then?" James asks as we turn down another road.

"Oh, a good hour I think." I try to remember, but the look on James's face makes me think that it doesn't sound right. "I could have done it quicker, but I was wearing the wrong shoes."

"Right," James is still frowning and looks at my outfit. "Well, don't worry, they have shoes you can rent there."

I hide the cringe on my face as I think about renting a pair of trainers countless others have sweat in.

"Fab," I smile and lift my chin. "So, are we going to climb the rocks by the London Bridge, then?" I say, trying to think of any rock formations I have seen around London. Perhaps he's planned a romantic picnic for when we reach the top!

James laughs, "I knew you would be funny. I could tell from your ad." James opens the door to a big brown building. "This gym has great walls to climb."

I laugh in return and restrain from hitting myself. Of course he wasn't planning on climbing actual rocks.

I knew that.

~

Who ever invented rock climbing is a close relative of Satan, I'm sure of it. When James pointed to the wall (yes, it's a *wall* with tiny stones sticking out of it that you are supposed to be able to balance on as you climb to the top), I laughed.

"I know," he nodded. "It's not much of a challenge, you're probably used to a lot more complicated stuff."

"Of course..." I nod in return and try to subtly wipe the sweat off my forehead as my eyes travel up the extremely tall wall.

I hate heights. I'm not afraid of them really; it's more like full on terror.

The man with our gear fastens a harness around

James's waist and is testing it to see if it's secure. I got my harness on first and it has a similar sensation to a really uncomfortable pair of thong underwear I own. The strap is right up my bum, and I'm trying not to think of where it is going to go when I actually start the climb.

"Right well, ladies first, Natalie," James indicates the wall.

"Absolutely," I nod, "only I haven't done my– er– pre-climbing stretches." I stretch one arm to the ground, but it only makes it to my knee as the strap rides higher up my bum.

"Oh, alright. Well I can go first, then." James looks at our instructor who nods and steps back as James attaches himself to the first rock.

I watch in amazement as James's perfectly sculpted body climbs, higher and higher. At a rather tricky part he even switches to have his back against the wall to leverage himself up.

I try and hide my nerves at the prospect of climbing the wall, but I can't stop my body as it slowly starts walking backwards until I bump into a hard object.

Apologizing I turn around, looking into familiar blue eyes.

"Oliver?" I say in astonishment.

"Nice outfit." Oliver's gaze runs over my figure

hugging pants and lingers on the low cut top which fits like a second skin.

"What are you *doing* here?" I ask, and look around for any sign of Angelica. Maybe this is a hot spot for dates now.

"This is my gym." Oliver smiles but then looks at my harness and frowns. "What are you doing here?"

I stand up straighter and put my hands on my hips. "I'm here to climb."

"Really?" Oliver asks, and I note a tone of disbelief in his voice.

"Of course." I look at Oliver in his shorts and tight fitting grey t-shirt and have to remind myself not to drool. I thought he looked excellent in a suit; I should have known it only gets better the less he wears.

"I guess I never pictured you climbing." Oliver reaches forward and tightens part of my harness that was a little loose.

"I'll have you know I'm an expert climber."

He smiles wider while nodding his head, and I can't decide whether I want to kiss him or smack him.

"I thought you were on a date tonight."

"I am." I bite my lip as I remember James climbing on the wall.

His eyebrow raises with a skeptical look. "He took you to the gym?"

"We, er– both like to work out." I look at James upside down on the wall and can't help but be impressed. "And it's not that weird for a date."

Oliver also watches James before looking at me from the corner of his eye.

"I guess if I were taking you on a date I would have a different exercise in mind."

I blush at his suggestion, which causes a wider grin on his face.

"Where's Angelica?" I casually ask while studying the floor.

"I don't know," Oliver replies.

"I thought the two of you had plans tonight."

"It's a dinner with some prospective clients," Oliver shrugs. "I didn't feel like going and Angelica can get along fine without me when she needs to."

Hmm... maybe I *slightly* overreacted to his dinner plans.

"So you came to the gym?" I add, "for fun?"

Oliver laughs. "I thought you liked the gym."

"Oh yes, of course I do." I can tell he is mocking me. Well, I'll show him with all my athletic...*ness* "I'm just surprised when I find other people who love it as much."

"I wanted to clear my mind." Oliver looks from

me to James. "Though I can see now that coming here hasn't worked either."

My pulse races at his implication, and I find myself taking a step towards him, wanting his touch again.

Okay, maybe I definitely overreacted to his dinner plans.

I jump when I hear a shout from James declaring he is coming down, and we both turn to watch James being lowered to the ground.

"Wow, that was great," I say when his feet hit the floor and he walks over to us.

"Yeah, piece of cake. Is this a friend of yours?" he asks, nodding to Oliver.

"Something like that," Oliver replies while they size one another up. "Is this yours and Natalie's first date?"

"Yeah." James smiles and puts his arm around my waist.

Oliver doesn't miss the gesture and he drags his eyes to James's face. "What made you decide to go rock climbing?"

"Well, Natalie seems to love extreme sports," James replies.

My eyes widen and I can feel my face turn bright red as Oliver's mouth relaxes.

"Of course, extreme sports." He leans back on

his heels and crosses his arms as though he is starting to enjoy the turn of events.

"Right before we got here she was telling me all about the time she went snowboarding down the French Alps." James turns to me and smiles. "It sounded amazing."

Oh God, please kill me now.

"Yes, that does sound amazing. You should get her to tell you about the time she went skydiving–now there's a story."

Oliver's smile is way too arrogant for my liking.

"Well Evil Knievel, I do believe it is your turn." Oliver hands me the rope, but I can't meet his eyes.

James gives me an encouraging pat on the back, but I can't help looking at Oliver, who has a huge grin on his face. He stretches out his hand indicating to me to go ahead, and at his mocking encouragement I raise my chin and take the rope from his outstretched hand.

Right, I can do this. It didn't look that hard actually. I might even be able to make it to the top before James did; I mean I do weigh less, so it's simple physics, isn't it? I secure the rope into my harness and the instructor checks to make sure it's locked. I approach the wall and survey it, trying to map out a course.

Once I have decided on what seems to be the

easiest route, I take a tentative step towards the wall and put my foot on the highest rock I can reach.

I've come up with an ingenious plan: I am going to pick the rocks furthest from the one I am already positioned on, and then I should only have to step on about five to get to the top.

To begin I gather momentum and lift myself up onto the rock using my foot for balance. It is quite tricky to stay balanced on one rock when you have to try and get to another. My arms are already starting to shake as I lift my left foot to the highest rock I can reach. I count to three in my head and heave my body up-

Oh shit— I just hit my head on the wall. Bloody hell, it hurts! I look around to see if either of the boys have noticed but feel my balance wavering, so I turn around and cling to the wall again.

Right, the trick is to get it done as quickly as possible. The more time I wait here the more adrenaline I lose. I look for the next rock and put my right foot on it. I reach above and settle my fingers in a nook, count to three and heave again— except I only make it half way and have to desperately cling to anything I can reach to stay on the wall.

I'm now grasping at the rocks, pretty much sideways, with a strap so far up my bum I am pretty sure it has nowhere else to go. My arms are shaking,

and I feel the sweat on my hands, causing me to lose my grip on the rocks. I try to look at Oliver from the corner of my eye but can't move from fear of falling.

"You alright, love?" I hear the instructor yell. "Would you like to come down now?"

"Oh," I call back, "umm... yes please."

"Right, lean back off the wall, then with you feet still touching it, slowly walk down."

I was wrong; the strap could go further up my bum.

When I finally make it to the bottom I have to sit down to stop my legs from shaking.

"That was ahh... great." James comes over and runs his hand through his hair.

"Yeah, I was trying a move I learned in Switzerland," I indicate to the wall. "But you must need real mountain ranges to do it."

James nods but I see a puzzled look on his face. Oliver is standing behind him with his body shaking from suppressed laughter and I want to kick him, badly.

"So," I shrug, "how far did I make it up?"

"Oh, to about the big blue stone there." James points.

What? That's only about ten feet off the ground! I thought I was at least half way.

"Right," I say and rise to my feet.

"Well, shall we go and get a smoothie, then?" James asks as he takes off my harness and starts rubbing my arms. "It's always good to rub your body down to keep your muscles from tensing up, but you probably already know that."

My puzzled look falls on Oliver, but he has stopped laughing now. He watches as James's hand grazes the side of my breast when he rubs the inside of my arm. With a tightened look on his face he turns around and walks towards the change room.

I peer over James's shoulder and watch Oliver leave, but he doesn't look back, and once James is finished with my arms (I told him I would do my legs myself later, I mean, this is our first date), we head off to the snack bar.

I've decided the snack bar is my favourite part of the gym. It's full of all sorts of yummy things that are *all* fat free, so it's basically like you're eating nothing! I've had two very yummy bars and a smoothie, and I'm seriously contemplating a second one.

"So, Natalie." James puts down his seaweed drink. "What are your main interests, then?"

"Oh, well, I like pretty much everything." I readjust myself on the stool as my bum is still a little uncomfortable from the harness. "Sports, obviously..."

"So you like all sports?" James asks.

"Pretty much all of them." I wave my hand in the air. "I don't like to put limits on my abilities."

"Wow, that's great." James leans forward. "It's nice to meet a girl who likes to actually *do* something. Most girls I meet are happy just to sit with their mates in the pub and watch Grey's Anatomy at night."

I nervously laugh and look at the table. I love Grey's Anatomy. When George died I got a petition together to bring him back. So far, only Hank and I have signed it– but we are still holding out hope.

"I went on this portage trip last spring with my old girlfriend and she complained the whole time," James sighs and shakes his head. "But I bet something like that would be right up your alley."

"Oh absolutely, that's my favourite type of trip."

What the bloody hell is portaging?

"So, besides sports, what do you like to do for fun?" James sips his drink.

"Oh, this and that..." I run my fingers through my hair. "But, what about you? I know you share my passions for sports and work in a bar, but..."

"Oh well, that's pretty much my life." James leans back in his seat. "The bar's great because I can take off as much time as I need to do what I love. I'm planning to climb Elbrus is the fall. My goal is to climb Everest by the time I'm forty."

"Wow. That's really impressive."

"Yeah, well you have to have a goal, right?" James takes another sip of his smoothie. "Who knows, maybe you'll climb Everest one day."

"Who knows?" I smile.

"Hey James!" Someone yells from the other side of the snack bar. We look around to see a young guy waving in our direction.

"Oh, that's Mickey." James gets off the stool and grabs his empty cup. "I'll be right back, would you like another smoothie?"

I look at my empty cup but shake my head. "No, thanks."

As James walks away I catch myself looking around for Oliver. I think I see him over by the weight lifting area, but when the man turns around it isn't him.

I just don't understand men sometimes. The way Oliver looks at me and jokes with me, you would think he was interested. But then, there is Angelica. I'm not sure exactly what, but something is going on there. He's never once told me they weren't seeing each other, and if they weren't, wouldn't he let me know?

I shake my head as I realise I am sitting in a gym, on a date, thinking about someone other than the guy I am supposed to be thinking about. Something is wrong with this picture.

James is a nice guy though, and he is the most attractive man I have ever dated. I mean, his hair alone would put Patrick Dempsey to shame. And– not that I was staring or anything– but his butt is really cute too. But, even with all those good points, I can't help sitting on this stool wishing I was drinking smoothies with Oliver. I wouldn't need to pretend to like extreme sports with Oliver.

James approaches again with our jackets. "Here you go," he helps me put mine on. "So, Natalie, would you like to come back to my place?"

"Oh umm..." I stall.

"Just for a drink of course," James adds.

I look up into James's beautiful grey eyes, run my eyes over his luscious brown hair and make one of the hardest decisions of my life.

"I don't think that's a great idea," I say and pull my hair from my collar. "You're a really nice guy James, but I just don't think it would work out between the two of us."

"Oh," James grabs the front of his jacket, "I see. Well, if that's the way you feel..."

"I'm sorry." I reach out to touch his arm.

"No, it's better you say something now, I guess." James shakes his head in confusion. "We just seem so right for each other though. I mean your love of extreme sports..."

I quickly avert my eyes and raise my handbag onto my shoulder.

"The thing is James, you're gone a lot with your extreme sports," I point out. "And I can't just leave my job anytime I want. We wouldn't really see that much of each other."

"You're right," James nods. "But, I could always go away less? Put off Elbris until next year."

I shake my head. "Now James, what kind of person— no— what kind of *athlete* would I be if I asked you to do that?" I put my hand on his shoulder. "No, you go and climb those mountains for both of us."

"Maybe I could call you sometime?" James asks. "You could show me some more of those rock climbing moves?"

"Sure," I nod. "That would be nice."

When I get home and search portaging on the internet I know I have made the right decision. Who in their right mind would find it entertaining to lift heavy canoes all day and then paddle down the river with food strapped to your back?

WHITE LIES

To The Man of My Dreams,

I am convinced that I won't find you by any sort of rock formation.

Or in a gym.

Obviously, you wouldn't be somewhere where I wouldn't go, or else how would we ever meet? Maybe I should start looking in the mall, or the nail parlour?

Hope to be seeing you soon,

Natalie Flemming.

P.S. I'm not sure if you are up on all the current trends or not, but I've just found these fabulous fat free snacks that have been invented. Basically, you can eat all you want, and not have to worry about gaining any weight! Science is so intriguing to me.

Seven

At work the next day, Hank and Rachel are excitedly reading the new preliminary guidelines that Oliver and Angelica have put in place.

"It says here that if I have any ideas, I can approach the management team." Hank puts down the paper and looks at me. "I'm going to tell them my idea for 'The Insider'."

I roll my eyes and sit down at my desk. Hank came up with the idea for the 'Insider' on his second day here. Apparently it's a regular shoe, but flipped inside out; meaning the pattern is on the inside, and the outside is what the inside of the shoe usually looks like. The trouble is the only person the concept makes sense to is Hank.

I haven't told Hank and Rachel that I'm going to the meeting tonight yet. I also haven't told anyone what is going on between Oliver and myself. Not that anything is. Or isn't.

This whole thing is so confusing.

I managed to convince Hank that when he walked in on Oliver and me in the boardroom, I had tripped due to a faulty contact lens, and Oliver was helping me find it. I'm not sure Hank *entirely* believed me, but he hasn't brought it up since.

"What does this part mean?" Hank points to the end of the paper. "The divisional lines between departments will be blurred to accommodate growth and change."

I pick up the paper and read it again. "Probably that they want us to interact with the other departments more, so we know what's going on."

"Right," Hank steps back. "Well, Natalie you can handle the designers then."

"Hank, Anthony asked you out months ago!" I argue. "And plus he has a boyfriend now. It's only awkward if you make it awkward."

"He does? No one told me!" Hank frowns and then shakes his head. "It doesn't matter– I mean, we all know what he was *insinuating*."

Rachel and I make brief eye contact, and look away while Hank goes over to his irises and starts rearranging them.

I look for Oliver all day, but at lunch I overhear Claire tell someone that he is out for the day with another client. My mind fills with horrible thoughts about attractive female clients, and I send a quick word to heaven, begging that the client be a middle aged balding man.

On my way home from work I decide to treat myself, and pop into the hair salon. I intend to only get a haircut, but when I sit down in the chair the stylist isn't too impressed with my hair colour.

"Sweetie, it's like someone spilled a can of 'blah' on your head."

She eventually bullies me into putting honey coloured highlights in around my face, and I have to say, they do look spectacular.

I'm on a high from my new style and decide to pop into Liberty on a whim.

After much reluctance, the sales lady talks me into buying one hundred and fifty pound Kurt Geiger shoes. But, despite the ridiculous price tag, I know they will look divine with my dress tonight, and I decide that if I don't take a taxi later, then it's sort of like the shoes were on sale.

Okay, and maybe I'm looking forward to seeing Angelica's face when she sees how gorgeous they are.

I make my way back to the empty apartment with my new shoes to get ready for dinner. I've never been to Kings before, mainly because one meal is about the price of my entire food bill for the month. I root around in the back of my closet for my grey silk Vera Wang dress. I got it for eighty-five percent off, and it still cost me over two hundred quid; but, as I put it on I remember it was worth every penny. It is a floor length, single shouldered gown with little flowers attached to the one strap. After I shake out my new hair and touch up my makeup, I do a final spin in the mirror, and I'm very pleased with the results.

God, these shoes are a bit tight though, aren't they?

They probably just need a bit of working in, though I can already feel blisters forming on the back of my heels, and I begin to dread the seven block walk to Kings.

I walk outside my building but stop suddenly when I see Oliver leaning against a Mercedes, looking amazing in his black suit.

Calmness washes over me when I see him, and I can't help the smile that spreads across my face.

His eyes travel from my freshly done hair, right to my open toed sandals, and he misses nothing in between. I look down as the blush spreads to my cheeks, but then take a deep breath and meet his gaze.

"I thought we were meeting at the restaurant," I say.

"I thought you would be wearing some ridiculous shoes and might need a bit of a reprieve."

I do my own slow appraisal of Oliver, starting with his hair which he has styled back for the occasion. He has on a sharp black suit, crisp white shirt, and a deep red tie. Some I'm sure would call his look daring, but I think he could make a plastic bag work for him.

"How long have you been waiting out here?" I ask as a slight chill runs up my arms, though it could just be from the way Oliver is lazily admiring me.

"Not too long," he says as he opens the passenger door and gestures for me to get in.

When I pass him standing by the open door he places his hand on my elbow and helps me get into the car. His touch electrifies me.

The car is gorgeous– and I don't even usually notice these things, but it obviously cost a fortune. It has plush leather seats, a state of the art sound system, and one of those maps in the center to tell you where to go.

We drive the seven blocks quickly, and I dart my eyes to Oliver's outstretched hand as he continually shifts gears. I curl my fingers into my palm as my mind reels with what else Oliver could do with those hands. He doesn't say anything for the beginning of the journey, which makes me wonder if he is waiting for me to say something.

"Where's Angelica?" is the first thing that pops out of my mouth, but as soon as I say it I regret it. I mean, I don't want him to think I am jealous or anything. I also don't particularly want to discuss Angelica, but, at the same time, I really want to know what she would think if she knew Oliver had come to pick me up.

"She was having drinks with a client." Oliver puts his turn signal on and changes lanes smoothly. "She'll be joining us there."

"She's putting those social skills to good use again?" I try and joke, but when Oliver raises his eyebrows I can't help but wonder if I've gone too far. "Sorry, I just got the impression that she intimidates everyone into doing whatever she wants."

He smiles. "Angelica isn't so bad. She has her faults, a lot of them actually," he qualifies, "but she's very driven and successful."

"Right, she is successful." I nod my head and look at my hands. "But, at what cost?"

I look out the window hoping for inspiration for a new topic to fill the awkward silence.

"Sometimes success comes at a great cost." Oliver's low voice causes my head to turn. "I should know that more than anyone."

I bite my tongue; I desperately want to know what Oliver is talking about. I decide to swallow my curiosity since Oliver seems lost in his own thoughts, and we pull up outside the restaurant moments later.

As the valet approaches Oliver's door he puts

the car in park and turns to face me.

"You know, you're really something else, Natalie Flemming."

I smile at his teasing tone and shrug my shoulders. "A girl can try."

Oliver leans over the centre console and I feel his warm breath on my cheek. His kiss is soft and sweet on my cheek and my insides melt at the sensation. Abandoning all reserve I turn my face towards him. He responds without any hesitation and puts his hands in my hair, capturing my lips with a demanding force of his own. The drugging kiss makes me lose all sight of reason, and I tremble as he ends it almost as quickly as it started.

Visibly trying to compose himself, he runs his hand through his hair.

"Trust me, you don't need to try."

I open my lips to respond when a sudden gust of wind runs down my spine; the valet opens the door and extends his hand to help me get out of the car. Our moment is over and I'm at a loss to decipher what it means.

With regained control, Oliver comes around the car and places his warm, firm hand in mine as we climb the steps to Kings. I try and take it all in: Oliver, the kiss, his hand in mine, this place– it all seems too much. Of course I've read about this place, but I didn't think it would be this... *cool*.

My eyes are wide with excitement as Oliver asks the hostess about our table. When I see she is occupied with looking through the reservation book I casually lean over the table to get a look at who else might be dining here. I've heard a lot of celebrities come here, and I scan the pages to see if any are booked in for tonight.

At the bottom of the page there is a star with a name that looks like it could be Gordon Ramsay. I try to step higher on my toes to get a better look, but the hostess snaps the book closed and looks at me as if to tell me she's onto me. I smile and bat my eyes in Oliver's direction in what I hope is an innocent manner; he shakes his head and silently laughs at me while the hostess indicates for us to follow her.

As we approach the table tucked in the back I can see everyone is already seated, with Angelica looking very bored. Oliver puts his hand on the small of my back to indicate I should go first. Angelica shoots daggers at me when she sees Oliver's hand linger on my back, but I avoid her gaze and slip into my seat.

I was under the impression that it would just be Angelica, Oliver, and myself for dinner, but sitting quietly at the opposite end of the table are Carl and Anthony, both looking like they too are wondering what they are doing here. I wave and Carl nervously waves back.

"Did the two of you meet outside?" Angelica asks both of us, though I feel the question is directed to Oliver, and so I wait for him to answer.

"No, I gave Natalie a lift here," Oliver replies, and I can't help but feel a little shocked he told her the truth. But, Oliver seems to be immune to Angelica's intimidation.

"This place is so cool," I look around the room and lean in towards Carl, "I think Gordon Ramsay is here tonight."

"Really?" Carl asks and surveys the room looking for the celebrity.

I nod excitedly. "I love his cooking shows. Every time I make something at home I always scream 'Bam!' as I'm throwing the ingredients in." Well, I did that one time I made chicken parmesan.

"That's not Gordon Ramsay," Anthony frowns.

"What, he's not here?" I ask and look around the room.

"No, the chef who says 'Bam!'. That's Emeril."

"Anthony, I think I would know who Gordon Ramsay is," I argue.

"He's right," Carl nods, "Gordon Ramsay's the one who yells at everyone and says fuck a lot."

Oh, yes, that's right. Oh, I hate Gordon. He's so

mean and those people are only trying their best.

God, I hope he's not here tonight.

When my filet mignon arrives and I take my first bite, I gasp. It is the most delicious thing I have ever tasted. I would never have thought to put oranges on beef, but it's so good I decide then and there I will try them on everything from this point forward, just in case.

After the main course, I pop into the loo to make sure I didn't get any of the sauce in my hair.

As I come back from the bathroom, Anthony gasps from the table. "Oh, Natalie, are those new Kurt Geiger shoes?"

"Oh– er– yes," I say and look down at my horrendously painful, but beautiful, shoes.

"Oh, they're fabulous," Anthony exclaims and peers round the table for a closer look. "Now this is art," he says as he puts his hand under his chin.

"Bloody painful art, though," I exclaim; my feet feel as though they are about to explode. "Why do people make shoes that you can only manage to wear for about five minutes?"

Anthony clucks his tongue. "Natalie, hasn't anyone told you beauty is pain?"

I roll my eyes and take my seat again. "How can someone feel beautiful in shoes when all you want to do is cut off your feet when you wear them?"

Anthony scoffs but I continue, "And how could I possibly get anything done in these? The sales woman said I could wear them to work and then out at night time. I've had them on for an hour and my feet already permanently hate me."

"Yes, but comfortable isn't beautiful," Anthony argues.

"Why can't it be?" I reply. "There are lots of beautiful, comfortable things in this world. Look at this dress: it's gorgeous, it's really comfortable, and I got in on sale."

"Are they still selling last season?" Angelica asks from across the table.

I ignore the jab and shrug. "Maybe I just want it all."

Angelica raises her eyebrows in disdain, but thankfully says nothing.

Anthony and Carl quickly start a conversation about the shoe's design elements as the waiter places the desserts on the table.

It seems to be an assortment of all desserts known to man. They are beautifully decorated, some with flower petals, and others with simple sauces in intricate shapes of star bursts and ornate symbols. They've been placed on spiral stands and I have to put my hands between my legs in order to not reach out and grab as many as I can.

"Well, these look lovely," Anthony comments and reaches for a bite size cheesecake.

"Yes," Angelica peers at them and mutters, "I wonder if any are fat free?"

I roll my eyes at her comment but see Oliver watching me while fighting a smirk on his lips.

"Oh Nat, you should try this lemon meringue, it's divine," Carl sings as he raises his hands in the air as if he needs support.

"No thanks. I try and avoid anything lemony if I can help it," I say and peer at the other treats.

"Really? Why?" Carl asks while still devouring his tart.

"I only have lemons in my tea when I'm sick, and I always feel better the next day; it doesn't matter how sick I am." I pick up a strawberry mouse in a chocolate shell.

"So, why can't you have lemons now, then?" Carl has stopped chewing and frowns.

"Because, if I get overexposed to them, then I will become immune and my tea won't work when I need it too," I reason and take another bite.

Angelica widens her eyes and pinches her lips together, looking at Oliver.

I can tell exactly what she is thinking. I'm supposed to be helping them out with the new marketing campaign, and I've just told them overexposure to lemons makes you immune to their medicinal qualities.

But, I still say it's logical. And even if it's not, why risk it?

Feeling like a total prat I clear my throat and try and right the situation.

"So, about the new marketing campaign." I say. "I've been thinking a lot about it and I think I've come up with an idea that would work."

"Excellent," Oliver says with a nod of encouragement. "Let's hear it, then."

"Well, I thought maybe we should go green."

"Go green?" Oliver asks.

"Yes, it's all the rage now a days." I nod for emphasis. "My mum won't buy anything unless it's green." Which is true, she now refuses to throw anything out because she says she can find a way to reuse it. I would call it hoarding, but who am I to judge?

"And what does 'green' mean specifically– to shoes, that is?" Oliver smiles.

"Well, it means recycled, doesn't it?" I look around the table for encouragement, but everyone seems to look very doubtful. "We will make all our shoes from only recycled materials. If we still charge the average two hundred pounds per pair we make more profit with a quarter of the cost. And everyone will love it because it's the socially conscious thing to do. The slogan could be "Saving the Planet... one step at a time."

Anthony's eyebrows are raised so high I think they might disappear into his hairline.

"Get it? One *step* at a time. Because they will be walking. In Makka's shoes," I add in case they missed it.

I look over at Carl who has the most disgusted look on his face. "You want me to buy *used* fabric?" Carl spits out as his whole body shakes. "What, shall I go down to the charity shop and buy some old prom dress and glue on some hideous bows to make the shoes?"

"Alright," Oliver interrupts and Carl sits back in his chair, fanning himself dramatically. "As I said before, we are just at the concept stage, so nothing is concrete. It could be a starting point, get our brains working," he says to me, but I find his assurances slightly condescending.

It took me all day to come up with that idea.

"It was just a thought," I mumble.

I put down my tart and pick my napkin off my lap. The rest of the night I keep my lips firmly sealed unless someone asks me a direct question involving the budget or accounts. Oliver, taking note of my withdrawal, tries to coax a smile from me by draping his arm along the back of my chair, but not even that can distract me completely.

Angelica talks about some marketing ideas, but they mainly come from Oliver. She seems to have no problems with this, in fact, the more Oliver explains and reveals about the new line, the more she smiles and drinks him in with her eyes. Which doesn't make me feel better at all.

It was his stupid idea for me to be a part of this marketing team, and the first time I put myself out there I get a condescending pat on the back and a "good try". I told him this wasn't a good idea; I told him I hadn't done anything with marketing for years, and now I look like a total prat in front of everyone.

And my idea wasn't that bad. I mean, I would have insisted they *wash* the used fabric first, of course.

By the end of the night, the team seems very pleased with the progress and proposals made amongst themselves, and I force a smile onto my face when they look at me for encouragement. "Of course we will have to run these by the board members," Angelica says as we walk out the front doors onto the main street, "but I don't foresee there being any problems."

Anthony and Carl decide to go to a club they heard about which is right around the corner and quickly get on their way.

"I'll give you a lift home, Natalie," Oliver says and places his hand on the small of my back.

"No, I'm fine thanks," I reply.

"I brought you here," Oliver argues, "and I will take you home."

I bristle at his commanding tone and straighten my back slightly. I know it's not Oliver's fault that no one liked my idea, but my hurt pride is looking for someone to blame, and he is the closest thing I have to a punching bag at the moment. And to be perfectly honest, I'm still not impressed with Angelica and his involvement, or whatever it is that they are to each other. I know that Oliver isn't interested in Angelica, that he wouldn't kiss me like that if he was seeing her, but, it doesn't make me any less jealous. I look to his car and can see Angelica has got into the front seat with her hand draped over Oliver's headrest, waiting for him.

"It's okay." I say and step out of his grasp. "You seem like you already have your hands full."

His eyes narrow and he opens his mouth to argue but we both look at Angelica, who is watching us intently.

"Really," I say and take another step backwards, "you go ahead. I have a few things to do on the way home anyways, so..."

"Oliver, she says she doesn't need a ride,"

Angelica argues from the car, and pats the seat next to her own.

He steps towards me and lowers his voice so only I can hear. "What crazy notion is running through that head of yours now?"

I raise my chin slightly and try and give a nonchalant shrug, but as he continues to study me I lower my eyes to his broad chest to avoid his searching look. He mutters something under his breath before walking round the car and getting into the driver's seat.

"Would you like me to get you a cab, Miss?" the doorman asks as I stand there looking up the street.

"No, thanks." I sigh and take off my new shoes. "I'll walk."

WHITE LIES

To The Man of My Dreams,

I have found a fab place to have our wedding reception. You know, in case you were planning on asking me. No pressure or anything though, you can take your time.

Five months should be enough, right?

I only ask because the restaurant's wait list is like a century long but they had a cancellation for October 29th, so I might have told them to pencil us in– just in case.

Hope to be seeing you soon,

Natalie Flemming.

P.S. I have already told them that Gordon Ramsay is not to be there, and if I see even one lemon I'm likely to have a meltdown. They seemed very understanding.

Eight

I've been avoiding Oliver like the plague for the last few days. I still feel like a complete idiot due to my lemon rant, and I also can't help but be a little ticked off with Oliver himself. I mean, he kisses me with so much passion that all future kisses will be put to shame, flirts with me throughout the whole dinner, but then goes running off with Angelica at the end of the night.

Alright, it was just a lift home, but still. He could have gotten rid of her if he wanted to.

I have a brainstorming meeting today with the Marketing Department, and I have to say I'm dreading it. I would have called in sick, but knowing Oliver, he would have just postponed it until tomorrow. Time to bite the bullet, as they say.

When I walk in the boardroom I'm surprised to see everyone already sitting at tables set up to form a large square, including Malcolm, who got Spencer's job when he left the company.

In my seven years at Makka, I don't think I have ever seen the Marketing Department look so...

professional. Even Fred, Malcolm's right hand man, is sitting down and whispering something into Malcolm's ear. At the last board meeting, he showed up wearing his golf shoes.

I join Anthony, Carl, and the other department heads at the opposite end of the table from the marketing personnel. Everyone is quietly whispering amongst themselves, and I must say it's the first time I have seen Malcolm look really nervous.

"Right, if you could all take your seats," Oliver enters the room with Angelica closely behind him. "Now that everyone is here, we can get started." He passes my chair and gently runs his hand along my back. To anyone looking it would probably seem a friendly gesture, but his warm touch causes my heart to race.

"Although I met quite a few of you the other day, let me formally introduce myself. My name is Oliver Miles. I am president of Westcott Solutions, and have helped many companies, such as yours, who struggle with production and marketing. I help companies see their true potential and fulfill it. It will be tough. I don't want anyone to leave under the impression that these implementations will be easy," Oliver gathers the pile of papers in front of him, "but I hope the end result will be something we can all be proud of."

Oliver walks around and hands everyone a piece of plain white paper. "After a brief but telling introduction to the company," Oliver seeks my eyes, "I think we can all agree there are issues that need to be dealt with."

I dart my eyes around the table to see if anyone one else sees the implications he is making, but they all seem mesmerized with Oliver. As I continue to study him I know exactly what is captivating them. He has such an easy way of bringing people together. He's wearing a casual sports blazer with no tie, which makes him look relaxed and approachable, not to mention gorgeous. I look at Angelica, who is studying her nails and looking quite bored, and wonder why Oliver puts up with her.

Oliver holds up a single white piece of paper. "You work here— many of you have for years. I would like you to gather into small groups and discuss what you believe the problems are with Makka, and any suggestions for how to fix them."

The people from the Marketing Department immediately pair up with each other.

"Natalie, you can be with Anthony and me," Carl gestures for me to join in their discussion.

"Oh— er— okay, thanks."

Anthony is already scribbling on the blank piece of paper.

"What's this, then?" I ask, pointing to Anthony's drawing.

"It's a great new idea I've had for ages. Unfortunately, no one has seen the potential in it, but now they want change, so…" Anthony scribbles a few more lines and sits back to observe his work.

He passes the paper to Carl and me so we can have a look. The sketch is a cross between a boot and a sandal, but with only a loop to keep your toe in. The rest of the foot is fully exposed while the shaft is knee high.

"Note the undershot heel," Anthony points out, "they're on the comeback."

"Oh well, it's… umm… great Anthony." I smile weakly. "But how would someone's foot stay in that?"

"They'd manage." Anthony waves off the question like it's an unimportant detail.

"Oh," squeals Carl, "we could do it in tweed!"

"I don't know, I mean, this is good," I say, "but maybe we should focus on something someone might actually wear."

"Who wouldn't wear this?" Carl says in outrage. I grab the piece of paper and ignore Carl's death stare.

"You wouldn't want to wear that?" Anthony points to the shoe and looks offended.

"Well, not really." I shrug, but avoid Anthony's eyes. "Where could I ever wear it? I wouldn't even be able to walk in it."

Carl smiles while shaking his head and addresses Anthony. "She's so naive." Carl turns around to me. "Honey, you work for the shoe– not the other way around."

"Well, I wouldn't wear a shoe that would make my foot freezing and unbearably uncomfortable at the same time," I counter his snarky tone.

"Alright, well, what would you wear?" Anthony asks.

"Well, I don't know." I casually hide my twenty pound sandals under the table. "Something I could stand to walk in for more than an hour."

"Well, fashion models would wear this." Carl points to the drawing, as if this argument solves everything.

"Exactly," I argue. "And how are we supposed to make money when our main clientele is fashion models– who we give demos to for *free?*"

Carl lets out a noise of disgust and quickly turns his back to me. I can hear him whispering words of encouragement to Anthony about the drawing.

I roll my eyes at their behaviour and turn around to see Oliver sitting beside me. I have no idea how long he's been there, but judging by the smirk on his face he's probably been listening for a while.

"Coming up with some good ideas?" he asks.

"I– er– not really," I say and try to push the sketch back towards Anthony.

"You mean there aren't brilliant ideas in that beautiful head of yours?"

My hand automatically moves to my hair and I can't think of anything to say, so I just shrug my shoulders.

No one has ever called me beautiful before.

"Maybe we should put that overactive imagination of yours to good use," Oliver says, lowering his voice so only I can hear. When my eyes lower to his soft lips he smiles and adds, "you know more than you think you do."

"Do I?" I whisper. My head feels so light because of the closeness of Oliver's mouth. I think my overactive imagination is being put to *very* good use right now. I know I'm in a crowded room with all my colleagues, but I hear nothing, see nothing, besides Oliver.

He puts his hand on my shoulder and leans closer. "We'll see, shall we?" He's standing before I know what has happened, and I feel like I might never quite figure him out.

"Right, I think that is enough brainstorming for now," Oliver raises his voice while Malcolm and Fred are playing tug-of-war with the paper. "Shall we all have a turn saying what we've come up with?"

"I'll go first," Malcolm rises from his seat when he finally gets the paper from Fred.

"Brilliant." Oliver takes the chair beside me again and sits down. His presence next to me makes me nervous and excited at the same time. One part of me wants him to go and sit somewhere else so I can concentrate while Malcolm speaks, and the other part wants to know what cologne he's wearing.

"Well, Fred and I have come up with some bangers here," Malcolm says as Fred beams from his seat. "Though, I do feel as though we have a slight advantage over the rest."

"Not to worry, if we could just hear the ideas," Oliver prompts while casually placing his hand on the back on my chair.

"Absolutely. Well, the first one is for sandal straps."

"Sandal straps?" Oliver asks.

"Yes, the straps on sandals." Malcolm continues, "women have a hard time putting them on and taking them off with all those straps and buckles. I always have to help my wife with hers. So, we have decided to make them all Velcro."

"Oh God," Anthony mutters to Carl. "Did he really just utter the 'V' word?"

"You want to make the straps Velcro?" Oliver frowns.

"That's what I said, didn't I?" Malcolm shakes his head as though the rest of us are crazy.

"Right, well, getting away from actual designs," Oliver sits forward in his chair with his hands clasped together, "did you have any ideas for the direction of the company, new lines perhaps, new branding?"

"Well... no." Malcolm looks at his paper again. "We only got as far as the Velcro bit." Malcolm sits down and looks at Fred as though their lack of ideas is solely Fred's fault.

"Not to worry, we're still in the brainstorming stage." Oliver looks around the table. "Why don't we hear what Anthony's group came up with?"

Anthony seems shocked at being called on next. He cautiously stands up and touches his hand to his hair to make sure everything is in place.

"Well, we were playing with some ideas for a tweed boot. New style, new lines." Anthony has his fingers on the drawing and I can tell he is debating whether to show it.

"Right," Oliver says and runs his hands through his hair. "Any marketing ideas or perhaps a new direction for Makka?"

"Well... from the marketing angle we were thinking maybe an– er– exotic line."

I look at Anthony and frown. We never discussed anything exotic.

Oliver takes a deep breath and turns in his seat to face me, "Natalie, would you wear an exotic boot?"

It takes me a few seconds to register that Oliver is asking me a question, "Would I...?"

"Wear an exotic boot designed by Makka?"

"Er... well– no." My hands start to shake and the excitement from Oliver sitting next to me has quickly gone.

"Why not?" Oliver sits back in his chair with his arms crossed which causes the fabric of his shirt to tighten over his sculpted shoulders.

"I, ah, can't wear Makka shoes," I mumble.

"Why not?" Oliver presses. I'm pretty sure he knows his questions are making me uncomfortable, and I glare at him for putting me on the spot.

"They don't make them in my size, and I can't afford them." My face has gone bright red and I shrink in my chair a little.

"You've been cursed with fat feet." Carl squeezes my shoulder. "It happens to the best of us."

Oliver ignores Carl and stands up. "Why doesn't Makka make shoes that fit Natalie's feet, or shoes that she can afford?"

I can only pray this is a rhetorical question.

"Because... she doesn't have any good clothes to wear with them, anyways?" I hear Anthony say in what I'm sure he thinks is a helpful tone.

I shoot daggers at Anthony with my eyes and he puts on an apologetic smile and leans back in his chair.

"Well, I don't see everyone knocking down our doors to get our shoes right now, do you?" I argue. "I'm sorry I don't want to wear some shoe that will make my foot freeze, and I may not be the most fashion-forward person in the office, but I know a good thing when I see it. So maybe all these wonderful designs of yours are what need a little *revising.*" I push Anthony's sketch towards his outraged body.

"*This* is who we should be marketing to," Oliver points to me. "Career women who want a stylish shoe, but that won't break their bank or their back."

Oliver walks over to the board and points to a chart.

"These are the sales reported from Trend Shoes in 2008; they recorded a total gross sale of just over seventeen million pounds." Oliver flips the chart to reveal another graph. "These are their sales when they decided to put a line into Next for 2009, note a rise in nearly a quarter percent of their total gross sales." Oliver points to the chart and then turns back to the group.

"When you make quality, stylish shoes that are accessible to more people than just supermodels and the socially elite, your profit margins increase dramatically."

"So, what you're suggesting," Malcolm raises his hand, "is that we base our new line on *the accountant?*"

"Well yes, and no," Oliver amends. "Not just Natalie– all career women, predominately in their twenties and thirties. Fun, sexy females who want to look and feel good." Oliver looks at me and my stomach has a funny fluttery feeling in it.

Did he just call me sexy?

"Well, Makka has prided itself in the past on being an exclusive brand of the finest workmanship," Malcolm argues, a statement which I know is straight from our old press package. "Do you want to go… common?"

"Makka will still maintain its high level of workmanship, and of course it will still produce higher-end shoes, but we will develop a new line that is more affordable and accessible. And I would hardly call Natalie 'common'," Oliver argues, and my face goes a deeper shade of red.

Angelica stands next to Oliver and places her hand on his shoulder. "The Marketing Department will be the ultimate driving force in this adventure.

Of course the designs will be a selling feature; but, the marketing division must implement this new strategy. There will be an unveiling in a little over a month's time. Of course this will be closed to staff and guests only, as a trial run, but we go to press in six weeks."

Wow, six weeks. That's a pretty tight timeframe to come up with a complete new line.

"All departments will be subject to scrutiny in the next few weeks to determine whether they are working to help this new line, or hindering it." Angelica looks around the table, though I feel her eyes settle on me. "And no one has a free pass."

"Having said that, we are open to hearing suggestions from outside of the Marketing Department, so please do tell your colleagues to approach Oliver or myself if they have an idea or concept."

"Right, well. Jolly good meeting, then." Malcolm rises and starts to collect his things.

Malcolm is the first to leave, quickly followed by the other marketing personnel. I can't help but get the feeling they're just as uncertain about this new marketing campaign as I am.

To The Man of My Dreams,

I've become somewhat of a celebrity at work. They've decided to base the whole marketing campaign on what I would wear. At first I was terrified: went home and chucked all my clothes. I mean, if I'm going to be an inspiration I need to look my best, right?

But then I was only left with my Vera Wang dress and my costume from when I was Betty Boop for the fancy dress party last year. Fortunately I caught the rubbish truck at the end of the street and they were very understanding. They even helped me into the back to sort for my bags.

Hope to be seeing you soon,

Natalie Flemming.

P.S. You wouldn't happen to know of a cleaners that specializes in getting the smell of garbage out of silk, would you?

Nine

Being the sole inspiration behind a new fashion line is definitely not as easy as it sounds. It takes me twice as long to get ready in the morning, and nothing screams 'inspiration' at me from my closet. At first I tried to go for an artistic look, but I kept getting my art smock caught in the filing cabinet. Then I tried to go extremely fashionable, but everyone kept stepping on my feathered boa. In the end I went for my normal work clothes, and have been wearing unusual broaches that I picked up at a car boot sale last year.

Despite my fashion setbacks, the company seems to be doing surprisingly well. Anthony has finally adjusted to having his designs approved *before* they go into production, and he's even sought my suggestions for some of them.

"Would this be something you would be able to squeeze your foot into?" Anthony asked me this morning as he held up a pair of gorgeous black and pink hounds-tooth pumps.

"Anthony, they're gorgeous!" I grab the shoe and try it on. Miracle of miracles, my foot slides in nicely.

"I hope your department appreciates that we had to buy extra material," Anthony adds, "the bigger sizes are basically using double the fabric."

"I'm sure we'll make it work." I roll my eyes. "You know what this needs, though?"

"To be three sizes smaller?" he asks, and his nose wriggles with mischief.

"No," I playfully hit his arm, "a little buckle on the side of the rim."

"Oh," Anthony looks at the shoe again, "that might work, actually."

The departments seem to be working very well together, and I hear laughter around the office again.

But, no one can argue that the biggest transformation is definitely the new Marketing Department. Oliver has got them excited about their jobs again. As I walked by the other day, they were all sitting in a circle on the floor coming up with ideas for the Fall Line, though Malcolm was sitting in the corner with Fred, sulking.

Oliver stops by my office nearly every day to ask me my opinion on some new concept or angle they've come up with, but to be honest, I'm not sure what help I can offer. I know these brilliant ideas are in me somewhere; when Spencer was in charge and I wasn't supposed to be thinking of any marketing ideas they came to me constantly. But now, I try and think of helpful things to say or contribute, and despite Oliver's encouraging words I know it's all crap. Now that I look back, the recycled material idea may not have been one of my best.

"Natalie, I've entered all the receipts for last month," Rachel turns to me, "but do you have the paycheque stubs?"

"Somewhere, I saw them yesterday."

"Hmm," Rachel comes over and hesitantly moves some things. "You know, we should probably sort this all out."

"Yes, definitely," I nod. "I will pencil it in for next month."

Rachel clucks her tongue and crosses her arms. "You know my mother always used to say 'never put off for tomorrow what can be done today'."

"And I agree." I hold up my arms defensively. "Only, my chiropractor said I'm not supposed to lift anything heavy."

Rachel squints her eyes at me, "I didn't know you went to the chiropractor."

"Oh," I shift my gaze away from her, "well, I do. Six times a week."

"*Six* times a week?" Rachel asks.

I bite my lip and think hard. Is that too many times to go to the chiropractor? I've always wanted to go, but I don't like the idea of someone fiddling around with my bones.

"I mean... three times a week."

Rachel still looks suspicious but shakes her head. "Well, Hank and I can do all the heavy lifting."

I look at the mess on my desk and the floor and realise she's right. "Alright." I push back my chair but it stops when it runs over a pile of papers.

"Hank, you'll help, won't you?" Rachel asks and looks at Hank, who shrugs and nods his head. "We'll even stay late if we have to."

I roll my eyes at Rachel's attempt to delay going home.

"So," I look around the room helplessly. "How do you go about cleaning up seven years' worth of stuff?"

Rachel tisks and picks up the pile of paper that is under my chair. "You're as bad as my girls. You just have to start at one area and work your way over."

"Right, of course." I look from one corner to the other. "Er– where should we start first?"

"The bar?" Hank mutters.

We decide to start over by the filing cabinets; we make quite good progress between the three of us and are about half way done when we run out of file folders.

"Right, I'll go and get some, then," Hank

volunteers.

"I don't think so," I say as Hank tries to run for the door. "You'll stop at the coffee machine and we won't see you for hours." I step over the pile we have created at the door. "I'll go."

Once I get the file folders from the supplies cupboard I stop by the coffee machine to get some liquid medicine for Hank and Rachel. As I pour the cream into Hank's cup, I notice a hand come from behind me to grab the sugar, and I turn to see Oliver behind me.

"Coffee break?" he asks.

"Oh, these are for Hank and Rachel." I raise the cups to show him. "And you?"

"Well, I was planning on it." Oliver puts the sugar back down and looks at me. "Would you like to go to the coffee shop down the road and get a drink with me?"

"Oh," I say and look at the coffees in my hand. "I would, but I can't. We're cleaning the office today, and I can't really leave them to do it when it's mainly my mess."

Oliver nods, but I can't help but wonder if he thinks I am playing hard to get. "No problem. Maybe another time."

"Sure, that would be great," I say and look down at the cups. Perfect, I wanted Oliver to ask me out, and now that he finally has I have to say no because I'm cleaning. Sometimes the world is so unjust. "Well, I better get back or Hank will come and hunt me down."

I turn around to leave and then turn back to see Oliver still staring at me. I know I should talk to Oliver about what happened the other night. But, part of me is avoiding the whole conversation because I am worried he is going to say it was a mistake. And another part of me is still upset he ditched me.

"I–" I search his gaze for some indication of what he may be thinking but he gives nothing away. "I'll see you around."

I walk away and head back into the office and I suddenly don't feel as thrilled to be cleaning out the office anymore. I know I did the cowardly thing– I mean, I should have at least heard him out. Now I'll have to spend the rest of the afternoon listening to Hank complain that if he knew we were going to be cleaning today he wouldn't have worn leather.

"Here you go," I hand Hank the coffees and drop the file folders onto my now tidy desk.

"Was that Oliver I saw you with by the coffee machine?" Rachel asks innocently. Rachel isn't quite as forthright about Oliver as Hank is, but I can tell she thinks something is going on between us.

"Umm, yes," I say casually. "He wanted me to go for coffee with him, but I told him I had to clean this up."

"You what?" Hank asks in outrage. "You told him you couldn't go out because you had to *clean*?"

"Well, I do!" I say defensively.

"Natalie, I'm going to ask you a question, and I want you to be absolutely honest with me." Hank takes my hand.

"Er– alright," I reply.

"When's the last time you had sex?"

"I–" I stammer from shock, "it's been a while..."

"You can tell," Hank says matter of factly. "So as your friend I am going to say this as simply as I possibly can– get your ass out of this office and have a sodden cup of coffee."

"But– the mess." I gesture around.

"Hank and I will take care of it, won't we, Hank?" Rachel assures.

"I suppose– though if I knew I was going to be cleaning today–"

"Oh, for God's sake, would you like to wear my bloody trousers for the rest of the day?" Rachel's argues.

I shake my head and quickly walk out of the office before they change their minds. I make my way over to the Marketing Department to find

Oliver, but stop at the end of the hall when I see him talking to Angelica. I turn around to walk back to the office when I see her gently touching his arm. What was I thinking?

I start to slowly walk away, but then I stop. The old me would turn around and go right back to the office in order to avoid an exchange with Angelica. But, this isn't the old me. This is the new, happy, clean office, nice broaches, Natalie Flemming.

I turn around and walk back to where Oliver and Angelica are standing and cough to get their attention. Angelica turns her head and looks down her nose at me.

"Yes, did you want something?" she asks.

"Yes, I did." I move my gaze from hers to Oliver's. "I wanted to know if you would still like to have a cup of coffee with me."

A satisfied smile spreads across his lips. "Yes, I would. Did you finish cleaning?"

"No," I turn my body towards his, "but it can wait."

"Oliver, what about that meeting we were going to have?" Angelica argues and gives me a false smile.

"It can wait," Oliver replies, and Angelica looks stunned to be put off. They look at each other for a second and eventually Angelica scoffs.

"Fine." Angelica gives Oliver a disapproving

look. "I will see you tomorrow." She turns around and storms off.

I'm shocked to see Angelica act coldly towards Oliver, but even more surprised to see Oliver put his foot down with her.

He places his hand on my back and we start walking down the hall towards the lift.

I subtly try and look around to see if anyone is watching Oliver and I leave together. There's hardly anyone in view, though, and the ones who are around seem focused on their work. Which is probably for the best— obviously we don't want people to speculate about our relationship— not that we have one, per say. People should mind their own business.

But, if they are going to talk about us, I hope they call us 'Nativer'. It has a cool ring to it, like it could be some famous explorer.

I've always felt 'Brangelina' was a little weak.

Once we are in the coffee shop and I have my drink in front of me, I look up to see Oliver studying me.

"What?"

"Nothing." He shakes his head. "It's funny, because I feel like I know you, Natalie."

A sudden warm feeling has filled my stomach. "Well, what's so funny about that?"

"I've only known you for a little while." Oliver

frowns and continues, "yet, the people in the office have known you for years, and I don't think they really see you at all."

"Oh," I say, puzzled, and shift under his scrutiny.

"I don't understand how they can't see you."

"Oliver, about the other day," I hedge.

"Natalie, I'm not really sure what is going on here." Oliver lowers his voice and reaches for my hand. "I know what I would like to be happening, but I also have to remember that I am leaving shortly."

"Right," I say, and feel my heart sinking at the thought of Oliver leaving soon, "you and Angelica are off to Germany together soon."

"I know you have this notion in your head about Angelica and me, but it's simply not true." Oliver puts his other hand on mine and gently rubs his thumb back and forth. "Angelica is someone I work with, that is it."

I sit quietly contemplating this for a while.

"So if it's not that, then..." What's the issue? We kissed. We like each other. Can't we just move forward?

Oliver removes his hands and sits back in his chair and I can see him debating how to answer the question.

"My father has been a brick layer since he was sixteen. I had your typical childhood, my Mum took care of my brother and myself while my father worked day and night to provide. He wanted his sons to follow in his footsteps and my brother Edward seemed more than happy to oblige." Oliver looks out the window and sighs. "I wanted something more though. I never got to see my father because he worked so hard, and when I did see him I could tell how unsatisfied he was with life."

Oliver looks down at his hands before meeting my eyes. "I decided when I had a family I would be in a position to be around more, that I would love what I did all day so that when I was home I wouldn't be miserable the whole time."

I swallow the lump in my throat and nod for him to continue.

"To say my father disapproved of my choice would be an understatement. So I came to London by myself, with nothing to my name. I've worked from the ground up every day since then, and now ten years later I have a successful company, and I love what I do. But it is a cut throat world out there. If I relent, even for a minute, there will be another company right behind me willing to do what I can't."

"I want a life with someone; I want to make someone happy. But, I just can't right now. I've worked too hard and for too long to let it all go now."

I hear every word that comes out of Oliver's mouth. It would be so easy to let it go in one ear and escape out the other, but his words are locked in my head. Slowly and painfully repeating themselves over and over again. When I'm just about to suffocate from their brutality I freeze, and I look at the struggle that is etched on Oliver's features. He looks exactly how I feel– torn in two. He's always such a contradiction to me. Sometimes he's so focused that I think it would send his world out of alignment if his pen ran out of ink. Then there are other times, times when he is caught off guard, or swept up in a moment, that I'm not sure he would recognize his own face in the mirror. He thinks he needs to choose between work and love, but why?

"Who says you can't have everything?" I argue. "Lots of people have relationships and still run successful businesses."

Oliver leans forward and takes my hand again. "I know what other people have, and I envy them for it," he shakes his head while searching for the words, "but, it isn't like that for me."

Oliver gets up from his chair and pulls it over so he is sitting right beside me. He puts his arm over the back of my chair and turns to face me. "But, even though I know all of this, I like you Natalie. More than I probably should."

The warning sirens are going off in my head. The sensible part of me wants to shake my heart and really listen to what Oliver is saying. He's saying we have no future, that he won't commit to a long-term relationship. But then there is another part of me. Another part I can't pinpoint: but a part that *knows* me. *Knows* Oliver. And it is telling me to take a chance.

"You know what your problem is?" I shake my head and lean forward. "You think too much. Brilliance is both a gift and a curse, and this is coming from the world's number one over-thinker. I'm actually requesting to have it recognized as a medical condition, if you would like to sign the petition."

My words seem to break the seriousness of the moment, and Oliver smiles and looks down at my lips with a raised eyebrow. "So you think I'm brilliant, huh?"

There he is. The relaxed, fun Oliver that I love to be with. As I take in his charming smile I make my decision. He's right– we'll never know what we're capable of unless we try.

He can't offer me forever. In fact, I don't know exactly *what* he is offering me. Oliver is warning me. Asking me to walk away, but I can't. I'm not sure why, but looking into his eyes, seeing his own internal struggle, I just can't.

I lean over so my lips are a fraction of an inch from his and whisper, "You have your moments."

He captures my lips softly at first, and as I return the pressure with my own need he deepens the kiss with punishing intensity. The kiss is long and fierce and a shiver runs up my back again, but this time I know it has nothing to do with the cold air. It's all Oliver.

I break the kiss before it goes any further in this very public place, and sit back to try and regain my composure. Oliver reaches in his pocket and puts the money on the table for our drinks before reaching for my hand, and leads me out of the coffee shop.

On the way back to the office we stop at a window display, and I'm distracted by a lovely pair of cream sling backs. They're tucked away in the corner beside a fuchsia exotic print pump with confetti all around it.

"They're so pretty," I say and admire the soft giraffe print in a slightly deeper shade impressed on the fabric.

"Hmm," Oliver shrugs. "Aren't they a little plain?"

"No!" I deny profusely. "That's the beauty of them. They may not turn everyone's head, they're only for the worthy to notice."

"Really?" Oliver studies me and then the shoes.

"Sometimes things are so beautiful, but so overlooked." I look at the shoes and think of all the men who passed me by for someone like Angelica. Someone I wouldn't want to be even if I could. "I used to wonder why people didn't do more to get the attention they deserve— beautiful people from the inside out that get overlooked everyday because they aren't cut throat or overtly obvious. But recently I've been thinking— maybe it's the people *looking* that are in the wrong."

Perhaps sensing the intimacy of the moment, and my own vulnerability, Oliver leans over and gently brushes his lips on the top of my head, causing my heart to patter.

Smiling, I draw back to see him admiring me.

We walk to Makka holding hands and casually shoot each other sly smiles. Oliver reveals that the marketing team still hasn't had their breakthrough, but I assure him it is only a matter of time. I give him a few more ideas, but I can tell by his lack of enthusiasm that none of them will work. I just wish I could help him, but the more I try, the harder it gets to come up with ingenious ideas. Maybe Spencer was right and I'm just not that creative.

When we get back to the office, Oliver walks

with me to my door and I peek inside at the now tidy space. Hank and Rachel are huddled in the corner trying a little too hard to pretend they're really focused on something else.

"Very nice and tidy." Oliver nods.

"Yes," I grin. "Well, thanks for the coffee. Sorry I wasn't much help with the marketing stuff; I'm sure you'll whip them into shape."

Oliver nods. "Yes, I'm positive a new marketing genius is at Makka." Oliver winks and touches my arm before walking away.

I smile as he disappears rounds the corner; it's probably the girl with those cool purple highlights.

Once Oliver is around the corner Hank and Rachel pounce on me for information.

"We just had a nice chat," I say and sigh at their searching looks. "Strictly professional."

I turn away to hide the blush rising to my face while remembering our kiss.

"So, he didn't ask you out, then?" Hank asks, sounding disappointed.

"No, why would he?" I reply.

"Well," Rachel looks to Hank, "we just thought he might ask you to the Gala."

"Well, even if he does, I'm not sure I should go," I say.

"What? Why the hell not?"

"Well, we are working together," I argue, "and he's leaving soon." I try to sound casual as I raise the arguments Oliver told me, but I'm secretly desperate to know what Hank and Rachel think.

"So, if Oliver were to ask you to Makka's Gala you would say no?" Hank looks skeptical.

"I think it would be for the best," I nod.

He mutters under his breath and I can tell he wants to argue more but lets it go.

On my way home I sit back on the tube and think about what I would *really* do if Oliver asked me to the Gala. Not that I am expecting him to.

If though– just for arguments sake– he *did* ask me out, I would probably have to say no. I mean, I like him, and I do want to go out with him, but it's a work function.

No, I should say no. It's the professional thing to do.

Of course, if he asked me out when we were outside of the office, then we would just be two people that like each other going on a date. Or, if he asked me out *in* the office, but we planned to go out *after* work, then that would be fine too.

But, it's probably not a good idea to go to the Gala together. I mean, that would definitely be crossing boundaries.

Though, the Gala is scheduled at *night-time*, and I

already decided that if he asked me out and we went after work it would be fine. Technically, it would be after work, there would just happen to be a lot of work people there. But, obviously that can't be helped... I mean, even if we went somewhere else we are bound to run into someone from work.

So, if he were to ask me to go with him I should be able to say yes.

I'll say yes. If he asks me, that is.

So, that's settled then.

To The Man of My Dreams,

I've seen the most beautiful shoes in a shop window and I seriously want to buy them. Now, as a responsible person I thought it might be best to consult you first, my future husband, considering the shoes in question are the same price as a small used automobile.

I'm sure you would agree that cars are extremely overrated (and with the price of petrol it's really the sensible choice to buy the shoes instead), but it is only fair for me to ask you first.

Though, I do need to know what you think *fairly* soon as the sale is only on for another fortnight. Shall we say if I don't hear anything from you in the next few days I may assume I have your consent?

Hope to be seeing you soon,

Natalie Flemming.

P.S. I have included a picture of the shoes so you can see for yourself how fab they are!

Ten

The next day I anxiously wait to bump into Oliver. I've made several trips to the coffee machine, but I still haven't seen him all morning.

It's so typical that on the day he is supposed to ask me out he is nowhere to be seen.

Alright, in his defense, he doesn't *know* this is the day he is supposed to ask me out, but still.

I run to the shop at the end of the high street for lunch, but get my sandwich in a takeaway and eat in my office. I hardly taste the egg and cress as my mind races with the possible reasons for why Oliver hasn't stopped by yet.

This is all Hank's fault. If he hadn't said anything about Oliver asking me out I would be sitting in the pub with Rachel having a lovely lunch. Instead, I'm sitting in my office eating a soggy sandwich and waiting for a guy who doesn't know that today is the day he is supposed to ask me out.

When I reach for my napkin to wipe my hands I accidently knock my drink over and it falls right into my lap.

"Shit, buggery, shit!" I grab the napkins from inside the brown paper bag to soak up the liquid. The liquid quickly wins the battle and I run out of napkins, and still have sopping wet trousers.

I take a deep breath and stand up, dripping juice on the floor in the meantime. Waddling out of the office and heading straight for the loos, I round the corner only to bump into something solid, and stumble back. I look up and see a familiar pair of blue eyes smiling at me.

"Well, fancy running into you," Oliver smiles.

I smile back and momentarily forget about my soaking trousers until I feel the liquid running further down my leg.

"Sorry, I can't chat right now," I point to my front, "slight problem."

"Oh..." Oliver stands back and frowns, but I have a feeling he wants to laugh as he fights the smile forming on his face.

"It's juice," I say.

"Well, I did think you were slightly too old for the other kind of problem," he laughs.

I waddle past him into the ladies washroom and lock the door behind me. After I have stripped off my clothes and put them under the water to remove the stain, I move onto the hand dryer to take out the dampness. Finally, after about ten minutes, I decide they are dry enough and slide them back on, though they still feel slightly sticky from the juice.

I unlock the door to the washroom and open it only to find Oliver standing on the other side, leaning against the filing cabinet.

"You're still here?" I ask.

"I wanted to make sure everything was alright."

My hands start to shake and I suddenly feel light headed as I move uncomfortably out of the doorway.

"Good as new." My trousers swish as I walk past him and my face starts turning red.

"Right, good," Oliver nods and looks around and then back at me. He opens his mouth to say something and then he seems to change his mind.

"Was there something else?" I ask.

"No." Oliver runs his fingers through his hair. "Actually, yes."

Oh God, he's going to ask me. I know I've been waiting all morning for him to ask, but I still feel very nervous all of a sudden. He keeps looking around as if searching for the words.

"Well?" I prompt.

"Well, I was just wondering about something you said yesterday."

"Oh?" I frown as I try to think if we mentioned him asking me out yesterday. Though, I'm pretty sure I would remember something like that.

"I–"

"Oliver!" Angelica comes round the corner. She zeroes in immediately on my stained trousers and rolls her eyes. I quickly try to readjust my position to hide the stain, but it doesn't seem to help.

"Juice," I explain.

"Oliver, you're needed in the conference room to sign those papers." She turns and waits for Oliver.

"Right." He turns and starts to follow Angelica.

Okay, I guess he will tell me later– though I have been waiting all day...

"What were you going to ask?" I yell at his retreating back.

He turns around but continues to walk backwards. "It's nothing– I'll catch up with you later." With that he rounds the corner and I'm alone in the corridor with stained, damp clothes.

When Hank and Rachel get back from lunch I am already engrossed in my work again.

"So, Natalie," Hank sits on my desk while I am typing and has a huge grin on his face, "are you going with Oliver to the Gala?"

"I most certainly am not." I continue typing.

"Really," Hanks says, "and why not?"

"Because, he hasn't asked me," I reply.

"Well, why don't you ask him?" Rachel suggests from across the room.

I stop typing and turn my chair around.

"I can't ask him," I say and look from Rachel to Hank. "The guy has to ask the girl, right Hank?"

"Not anymore," Hank shakes his head, "nowadays it's a free for all."

"Really?" I ask skeptically.

"Absolutely, the lines that were once drawn have been erased," Hank nods knowingly.

I think we might have shot ourselves in the foot a bit with this women's liberation business. Now men have even less work to do in the bloody relationship.

"Well, it doesn't matter," I turn around and start typing again, "because Oliver and I are just friends." To be honest I'm not sure what we are, but I'm obviously not going to admit this to them.

I hear Rachel snort from across the room and swivel around in my chair again.

"What?" I ask.

"Well, anyone can see you're not 'just friends'," she argues.

"Well, *anyone* would be wrong, because we are just friends."

I look up at Hank who has a pitying look on his face.

He puts one hand on my shoulder. "One word for you honey: denial."

"I'm not in denial!"

"So you're saying you don't like him?" Hank asks.

"Of course I like him," I shrug. "What's not to like? He's nice, thoughtful, attractive, a good person."

"A good person." Hank mimics in a high pitched voice– which doesn't sound like me at all– and shakes his head.

"Do you *like* like him?" Rachel has come across the room and stands in front of me.

"I-" I look at the wall and shrug. "Maybe."

"She *like* likes him!" Hank squeals.

"So why don't you go and ask him to the Gala, then?" Rachel argues.

"Because... I'm not entirely sure he *like* likes me?" I study my fingernails and think about all the arguments Oliver brought up about our relationship being a bad idea.

"Oh honey," Hank grabs my arm to make me stand up, "there's not a doubt in anyone's mind that he *like* like's you."

"Can you stop saying *like* like?" I argue.

"No, it's more fun this way." Hank smiles and opens the door.

I look from Hank to Rachel who are both staring at me.

"Well?" Rachel asks.

"Well, what?"

"Go and ask him." Hank gestures to the hallway.

"Right now?" I look at the pile of work I have on my desk. "I can't ask him right now, and I'm still not sure this whole thing is a good idea."

"Oh for God's sake," Rachel grabs my hand and leads me out of the office. "When you get to my age you realise that anytime is a good time."

I look behind and see Hank is following us with a very excited look on his face.

"Honestly, you two, this is a bad idea." We walk past Reception and into the west end of the office. "What if he says no?"

"He won't say no," Rachel argues.

"But what if he does?" We stop outside of the Marketing Department, and I look at them both with reservation. I'm not sure I could handle another rejection from Oliver. And there is no way this time could be a misunderstanding or an off-handed suggestion. "I won't be able to face him again if he says no."

"Natalie, I promise you he will not say no." Hank puts his hand across his heart.

I look into the Marketing Department and can see Oliver in his office. I sigh and turn back to Hank and Rachel. I know what Oliver said at the coffee shop– that he's not ready for a long-term commitment. But, he did kiss me, so maybe he does like me more then he's willing to admit. My gut instinct tells me this is a bad idea, but I quickly tell it to be quiet. When I knock on the open door, Oliver looks up and smiles.

"Hello, Natalie."

"Hi Oliver," I say and walk forward. "I hope I'm not interrupting, I just wanted to ask you something."

"Always so polite," I hear from behind me and turn to see Angelica sitting on the chair inside the door.

"Hello Angelica," I nod, "I didn't see you there."

"Clearly." She rises from her chair and stands beside Oliver's desk.

"You wanted to ask me something?" Oliver puts down his pen.

"Oh, right yes." I look from him to Angelica.

Obviously I can't ask him now, not with Angelica watching.

"You know what, it was actually nothing." I wave. "I can just ask you later."

"Well, you came all the way here," Angelica smiles, "so it must be *something*."

God, what a bitch.

"I mean, unless you make it a habit of walking the halls for no reason?" Angelica frowns and I secretly hope the lines permanently stay there.

I have a right mind to ask Oliver out right in front of her. It's about time someone put her in her place.

Though, I was hoping it would be someone else.

"Actually, I just wanted to have a quick word with Oliver about the Gala," I smile.

"Oh, yes, the Gala. Won't it be sensational?" Angelica purrs and sits on the end of Oliver's desk.

"Yes, I'm sure it will be." I turn my attention to Oliver. "So, Oliver, I was wondering–"

"I'm having Anthony design the most fabulous shoes for my dress," Angelica interrupts. "I mean, Oliver looks fantastic in his suit, so I will need something extra special to stand out on his arm." She laughs, but it sounds more like a cackle.

My heart sinks as what she is insinuating sinks in.

"Oh, so you two are going together?" I ask, looking at Oliver.

"Representing Westcott Solutions," Oliver replies and I can see he wants to add more, but with Angelica sitting there he decides not to.

"We attend all these functions together. It's great for the company. Oliver says it shows a united front." Angelica gets up and walks to the front of

Oliver's desk. "Well, I better check on Anthony and see if he has anything for me to review. Great talking to you, Natalie."

I nod as she walks past.

"Natalie," Oliver says and stands up, "I hope you don't mind that Angelica and I have to go together." Oliver is studying my face, waiting for me to answer.

"Mind?" I say but avoid his gaze. "Why would I mind?"

"Well, I thought maybe you were coming in to ask if *we* could go together." The fact that he knows why I came here just makes the whole thing more embarrassing. Well, if he thinks I'm just going to sit alone at the Gala, pining for him, he has another thing coming.

"You thought–?" I give a breezy laugh. "No, I was– er– actually seeing if I was able to bring a date."

"A date?" Oliver frowns and folds his arms across his chest. "You want to be bring a date?"

"Yes," I say and lift my chin and meet his eyes, "would that be alright?"

"It's just–" Oliver clears his throat while his jaw tightens, "I wasn't aware you were still seeing that guy from the gym."

"It's someone else." I run my finger over the corner of his desk.

Oliver quietly studies me, but I'm proud to say I reveal nothing. Just when my eyes start to water from not blinking, I finally hear Oliver reply. "Fine," Oliver comments in a low, tightly controlled voice, "bring your date."

"Fine," I reply, "and have fun on yours."

"It's not–" I turn around and walk out before Oliver can finish. I fume all the way back to my office and slam the door closed once I'm inside.

"How did it go?" Rachel leans forward and smiles.

"He's going with that bitch Angelica," I sneer and collapse in my chair.

"But, he can't," Hank argues.

"Well, he is," I take a deep breath, "apparently they go to all of these functions together."

"Oh, Natalie, I'm really sorry." Hank touches my shoulder, but I pull my chair in closer to my desk and pick up the papers I was working on earlier.

"It doesn't matter," I say and flip my hair over my shoulder.

"Well, we can go together, then." Hank sits on my desk.

"Actually, I have a date, but thanks anyways."

"You do?" Hank frowns. "But then why were you going to ask–"

Hank suddenly stops as Rachel clears her throat

loudly.

Hank stands up and I continue typing on my computer where I left off. The funny thing about anger is it usually turns into tears quickly after, and I can already feel some brimming at the back of my eyes.

"Well at least he didn't say no," I hear Hank say to Rachel as the first tear finally falls over my lashes.

EMILY HARPER

To The Man of My Dreams,

I've decided I am rebelling against women's liberation. That's right- you heard me. I'm not putting any matches to my bra, in fact, I think I might look for something with *extra* padding.

This means that you are now responsible for all aspects of the relationship which involve rejection. This includes all date requests and any marriage proposals.

Hope to be seeing you soon,

Natalie Flemming.

P.S. I also lost my best pair of panties today to a vicious attack from a glass of grape juice. Needless to say it's been a trying day.

Eleven

The next day I sit at my desk after Hank and Rachel have left for the day, trying to figure out where everything has gone wrong. None of my dates have gone according to plan, and I can't figure out why.

And then there is Oliver.

Alright, if I am being completely honest I would say that the dates didn't go very well because Oliver ended up being there. There is just some sort of strong, inexplicable connection between the two of us, and when he is in the room it's like no other man can compare.

He tried to tell me, to warn me, but I didn't listen. I didn't want to listen because I just wanted Oliver. But, he doesn't want me. He chose his business and Angelica, and I refuse to sit around and think of all the things I could have done differently.

Besides, I did that all last night and it is way too depressing and I've run out of tissues.

Just as I'm about to pack it in for the day, Carl comes rushing in my office clasping his chest and gasping for breath.

"Oh– Natalie– thank God– still here. Slight crisis," he takes a deep breath, "come quick."

Panicking I grab my handbag and run after him. God, I have been training for this my whole life. I took the first aid course three times– I didn't *technically* fail the first two, as I don't feel the CPR doll's head should come off quite so easily. Whatever the case, with my certificate in hand and frantically trying to remember if I am supposed to compress the chest to the beat of "Staying Alive" or "Dancing Queen", I know that if someone needs the kiss of life I am their girl.

I run into Fabrication behind Carl and desperately look around for someone dying. I frown when all I see is twenty shoes lined up on the table with Carl collapsed beside them.

"What's wrong?" I look around again. "Who's dying?" I hear the doors open behind me and turn to see who has come into the room.

"Anthony, I'm sure we can–" Oliver stops when he sees me. His jaw tenses and he looks at the wall, putting his hands in his pockets.

I raise my handbag higher on my shoulder and firmly place my chin in the air. Two can play this game.

"What's going on?" I turn to Anthony who has also joined Carl at the table.

"It's our babies."

"You have babies?" I ask. I didn't even know they were seeing each other.

"No," Anthony indicates the table, "these babies."

I look to Oliver who has casually walked over to the table, keeping his back to me. Always the professional, isn't he? He hasn't even looked at me since he walked in, focusing on Anthony and the shoes instead.

"Am I missing something here?" I ask and walk to the other side of the table, turning my body away from Oliver's. If he wants to be childish then so can I. I *invented* childish behaviour.

"The marketing team cocked up again. They were supposed to do a brochure for the shoes to give out at the Gala, but they haven't done it." Carl shakes his head in disgust. "How could they not have done it?"

I look at the shoes that line the illuminated table and can't help but be impressed. I knew everyone had been working really hard on the new designs for the Gala, but I never imagined they would look this good. And even though they are some of the most simple shoes Makka has ever made, they look both stylish and comfortable.

"It's not like they weren't planning to do the

brochure." Oliver turns to Carl to defend the department he has been working with so closely. "With all the staff layoffs, the department has been reduced to basically nothing. We don't have the manpower or resources to do the brochure. And it's not like we've been getting much input or help from the rest of the departments."

His words cause me to take a quick intake of breath. How can he even say that? I tried multiple times to help him out with his campaign; anytime I opened my mouth he gave me a condescending smile and told me to "keep trying", like I was a child he was trying to placate.

"And that's my fault, I suppose?" I straighten my back and turn to face Oliver. "I wasn't even told about these brochures until now, so how can you say that I didn't contribute to them, or approve the resources?"

"I didn't say you didn't approve the resources." Oliver places his hands on the table and leans forward. "But now that we're on the subject, I wouldn't think you would have a problem with it considering you seem to have enough *resources* all over the place."

My lips tighten at his words and I lean forward on the table as well. "And what is that supposed to mean?"

"Nothing," Oliver shrugs, and I can see the suppressed anger in his face. "Just that maybe people are getting a little confused about which *resource* you are going to approve next."

I take a deep breath and try to control the rage that is boiling inside of me. "Oh, is that so?"

"Alright, let's not get our knickers in a twist," Carl laughs while carefully taking in our angry faces. "Even if we had the resources, who would make the brochure with such little time left before the Gala?"

"Good question Carl, because I sure don't know how Oliver will ever be able to decide."

His eyes narrow. "I would choose the person most suited for the job on a professional level. I have to leave my personal feelings out of it."

"Oh of course, the most suited for the job," I say and clench my fists at the side of my thighs. It's so easy to say that in theory, but I didn't get the marketing position from Spencer when I was most suited, did I?

Anthony's eyes widen and he and Carl's heads bounce back and forth between Oliver and myself.

"Sometimes, you have to do things that you don't want to do for the greater good of the company." Oliver shakes his head in exasperation. "If you lose sight of that you're not only putting your company at risk but all the employees that are depending on you. I don't see why it's so hard for you to grasp that you have to make sacrifices that take you out of your comfort zone, and perhaps away from your personal wants and needs, to reach your ultimate goals."

"And what goals are those again?" I yell in frustration. "Oh yes, be the most successful person on the planet just to rub it in your dad's face. And then what? What will you do after you've reached this unattainable goal and realise that you've ended up all alone?"

"You don't know what you're talking–"

"Actually, for once I know exactly what I am talking about."

"So what do you want me to do, then?" He throws his arms in the air. "Pack it all in and forget everything I've worked for? Can't you see I've come too far– that I don't have a choice?"

I shake my head as my chin wobbles a bit, trying to hold my emotions back. "Actually, you do have a choice, and you made it."

I turn my face away from his as I feel the tears brimming at the back of my eyes. God, I would give anything to be able to walk out of this room without him seeing me cry.

"Natalie– I," Oliver runs his hand through his hair in bewilderment, "I don't know what to say, what to do to make this right."

I sniffle a bit and take a deep breath. "You've said all there is to say, let's just leave it at that."

As we stand in Fabrication, me staring at the ground, Oliver staring at me, and Carl and Anthony desperately trying to stare at both of us at the same time, an awkward silence fills the room.

"So, about the brochures then," Anthony hedges.

"I will make sure to outsource them and have them in time for the Gala." Oliver replies.

"And send me the bill and I will put it through," I quietly respond. I turn and walk out the door, hoping to put as much distance between Oliver and myself as possible.

When I am only a few steps down the hallway I feel a hand grab my arm and spin me around. Oliver gathers me into his arms, and presses his lips to mine with a kiss that is long and fierce. The anger that I felt in the room is washed away with an intense desire to hold onto him for as long as I can, trying to remember these last precious seconds together. The pressure of his mouth washes away all my defenses until I am left raw and exposed in his arms. When he finally pulls back I can still feel the heat from his lips on mine and I have to remind myself to breath in and out.

"Natalie, just because I can't give you what you want doesn't mean I don't care about you," he argues.

As I look into his eyes I want to forget about everything so badly. I want to pretend like I don't care about the happily ever after, that I'll take whatever Oliver can give me, for however long he can.

"I can't," I say and push out of his arms to create space between us. "I want more. I want it all."

Oliver nods and withdraws his hands from my shoulder. "I know you do, and I wish to God that I could give it to you, but I can't."

I search his eyes and can't understand how he can't see what I can see. That everything he wants is just a stone's throw away. "It's not a matter of can't. It's a matter of won't."

I step back, completely out of his grasp, and it feels like there is a great big valley dividing us instead of the few feet of carpet. I turn to walk away, and Oliver doesn't try and stop me.

I attempt to control the tears that are falling down my face and reassure myself I am better off without him. He made his choice and now I have made mine. Sadly though, words and logic never seem to work on a broken heart, do they?

The minutes tick by into what feels like hours, and I finally get myself together enough to collect my things from around the office. After I gather my purse and coat I race to the lift as the doors are closing, wanting to get out of the building without having to speak to anyone else. I put my foot between the closing doors in order to open them only to see Angelica standing in the lift looking at her Blackberry. I pause for a moment to contemplate taking the stairs, but even with my blotchy tear-stained face I just can't stand the thought of her thinking she's won. Silently cursing, I give a polite smile and try to pretend that my world hasn't just collapsed. When her eyes lock with mine a satisfied look comes on her face and she quickly puts the Blackberry in her bag.

"I must say I have really enjoyed working here for the past few weeks," her casual remark makes my whole body tense. I knew it was too much to hope that the elevator ride would be silent. "It's so refreshing to see a different kind of life every now and then."

"Mmm," My fingers itch to scratch her face, and I regret it as soon as the question starts flowing from my lips: "And what different kind of life is that, exactly?"

"Oh, you know how it is," she laughs. "Life is

just one fabulous party after another; sometimes it's nice just to have a change of scene."

My eyes narrow on the lift buttons and I desperately try to count to ten.

"You know, Oliver wasn't always the prestigious businessman he is today. He can wine and dine the clients like he was born with a silver spoon in his mouth, but he knows exactly where he came from," Angelica sighs in content, "and that's why he never wants to go back."

I look at her from the corner of my eye, and even though I want to kill her, I can't help but feel sorry for her. Even after all this time she still doesn't see who Oliver really is, what he's capable of. She sees how handsome and rich he is and what he can do for her, but she doesn't really know him at all.

She doesn't know the Oliver who has that mischievous look in his eyes when he's supposed to be serious but he can't help but laugh, or how his leg bounces slightly when he gets excited about an idea and is waiting to explain it. She doesn't know the passion he feels when he talks about his job and his client's success.

She may socialize with the elite, but in life and love she is a very poor woman.

"I'm very much looking forward to the Gala." Angelica clasps her hands together. "I'm planning a very special night for Oliver and myself."

"I'm sure you will have a lovely time." I press my lips together and inwardly scream at how slow the lift is moving.

"I plan to make it a night Oliver will never forget." Her malicious smile spreads across her face and I can't hide my look of disgust any longer.

The lift doors finally open to the main lobby and I don't even try to be polite– I race ahead of her to get out.

"Natalie?" she calls and I have no idea why, but I stop and turn.

"Yes?"

"It would never have worked between you and Oliver. You know that, right?" She walks to stand beside me as she puts a leather glove on one hand and then the other. "I know he has a little infatuation with you, but ultimately he loves his job more than anything. He would be a fool to think he could have both."

"Doesn't that bother you, Angelica? I mean, you obviously are looking for something more with Oliver, so doesn't it upset you that you would always be second to his career?"

"No." If she didn't say it with such assurance I would think she was bluffing. "Unlike you, I live in the real world. I haven't disillusioned myself with some silly notion of a fairytale romance. What Oliver and I would have would be satisfactory for both of us, I wouldn't get in the way of his career, and his success could do things for me both professionally and personally that would take me years to accomplish on my own."

My hands are clenched at my sides and my anger has finally reached its boiling point.

"You're a very sad women, Angelica." I don't wait to see her reaction as I turn and quickly walk out the building.

To The Man of My Dreams,

    Now, I don't want to rush you or anything. I mean, of course I know we need to meet when the time is right. But, if you should happen to feel the time is right around— say 6 o'clock tonight— that would be fantastic.

    I've got myself in a little bit of a sticky situation— nothing I can't handle of course...

Hope to be seeing you soon,

Natalie Flemming.

P.S. Don't worry about a tuxedo. I think Hank still has the one he wore as James Bond last year.

Twelve

Alright, this is it. No more messing around. I've been sulking around the office for the past few days and even I'm getting worried about myself.

Hank and Rachel try and be encouraging– well, at least I think that is what they are trying to do– but it isn't really working. Hank's idea of trying to get me to forget about Oliver is to criticise him any chance he can get.

"Did you see him help that lady in the wheelchair this morning?" Hank sneers in disgust. "Can you say 'trying too hard'?"

Only, his criticisms aren't very helpful.

Rachel is trying to offer support by bringing in chocolate for us to snack on. Anytime one of her children calls or she thinks I look upset, she brings out another box and we quickly make our way through it.

So, my pants are getting tighter, I have no date to the Gala, and Hank's critiques only make me like Oliver *more*.

The Gala is tomorrow and I'm starting to worry

I will have to admit defeat. I even tried searching the bin for James's number until I remembered I threw it in the trash on the way home that night so I wouldn't be tempted to call him. He's probably too busy climbing bloody Mount Everest anyways.

I've avoided Oliver since our terrible blow-up in Fabrication. He hasn't tried to find me either, even to talk about anything related to the marketing campaign, not that I care. Obviously I am better off without him.

I mean, it wasn't like I was asking for a marriage proposal this instant. But, I'm also not going to convince someone to love me. I have *some* self-preservation.

~

The Gala is in less than five hours and I still have no bloody date. To make matters worse, Hank has been prancing around the office all day with a huge grin on his face because he thinks he's my bloody knight in shining armour, when all he did was royally screw me over.

Jerry, from Marketing, stopped by our office this morning to let me know that the new brochures were arriving this afternoon and they needed a cheque printed for when they get here.

"Umm... Natalie... You know I was just

wondering..."

"Yes?" I said and looked up from the invoice he'd just handed me.

"Well, I was wondering if you were going to this Gala tonight."

"Oh– er– yes." I turned my chair to face Jerry, and he stood awkwardly in the door avoiding my gaze.

I could feel Hank standing behind me, watching the exchange closely.

"Well, the thing is," Jerry swallowed the lump in his throat, "I was wondering if perhaps... you would like to go with me?"

I smiled at Jerry and felt like I was really seeing him for the first time. He's not the most attractive bloke in the world, but he has a round friendly face and his hair is neatly combed. He could stand to lose a few pounds round the middle, but who couldn't?

"Wow, Jerry, that's really sweet." I stood up. "I would love–"

"She can't," Hank interrupted.

I turned around and opened my eyes wide in an attempt to tell Hank to shut up, but he just winked at me.

"She has a date." Hank stepped in front of me. "And you can tell your boss that and all."

"My–" Jerry sputtered.

"You heard me!" Hank poked Jerry in the chest. "Now get back to where you came from."

Jerry looked around widely in disbelief, as if someone was playing a joke on him, but Hank placed his hands on his hips and started tapping his foot.

"Right, well," Jerry scratched his head, "see you tonight then."

I stared at the floor where Jerry was standing and was too stunned to say anything. That was my chance. Someone had asked me out.

"You're welcome." Hank patted my shoulder as he walked by and went over to Rachel's desk to give her a high five.

Of course I couldn't say anything to them; they think I have a date for tonight. And I know they are only trying to help, but I still can't help but want to kick Hank when he skips over to my desk and hands me the cheque for the brochures.

"Natalie, would it be alright if we left a little early today?" Hank asks. "Only, we wanted to get ready for the Gala."

"Oh– er– sure, go ahead," I wave, "I think most people have already left anyways. I'll just go and pop this cheque over to Marketing and I'll leave too."

Rachel comes over and places a hand on my shoulder. "Would you like me to take it?"

"Oh, no that's fine." I shake my head and try

and reassure them as I see their worried faces. "Oliver left at lunch, I saw him go. I'll be fine."

"Alright," Hank buttons his coat, "but if that Jerry gives you any more trouble, you let me know."

I smile. "Will do."

Actually, Jerry is the reason I'm dropping off the cheque. I had a genius idea about an hour ago that if I caught Jerry before he left, we might still be able to go to the Gala together.

I wait for Hank and Rachel to disappear around the corner, and then practically sprint to Marketing. The place is deserted. I look around the office to make sure Jerry isn't hiding in any corner, but after a few minutes concede he must be gone.

"Someone order pamphlets?" A man enters the room carrying boxes.

I remember the cheque in my hand and realise these must be the brochures. "Oh, yeah, they're for tonight."

"I need someone to sign for them," the man comments and looks at his clipboard. "And it says here that you're supposed to cover the shipment."

I look around the office. "Well I can sign for them. Do you work for the delivery service?" I ask him since I notice he isn't in uniform.

"Actually, I designed the pamphlets." He points to the one I'm holding. "The delivery guy is sick today, so I got the job."

"Oh," I smile, "well they're great, thanks for getting them over here."

"Not a problem. I'm Nick by the way." Nick extends his hand and I shake it.

"Natalie," I reply.

"Well, it's nice to meet you, Natalie." Nick attaches the pen to the clipboard. "Have a nice time at your party tonight."

"Thanks." He turns to walk away and suddenly a crazy thought pops into my head.

"Hey, Nick. Are you doing anything tonight?"

~

I rush into the flat, throwing the brown package that is sitting on my doorstep onto the hall table, and run straight into my bedroom to start getting ready.

Luckily I put together my outfit the night before, just in case I got caught up at work today. I bought a special dress for the evening, which cost me more than I make in a week. Hank thought it would be a good investment though, as he said I could wear it to his wedding someday.

I run my fingers over the beautiful pale pink chiffon and feel a flutter in my stomach. I've tried it on every day this week for a morale booster, but it is still more exciting when you know other people are going to see you in it. The beautiful crystals on the bodice sparkle under my bedroom lights.

Catching sight of the brown box in the mirror I frown in concentration. I don't remember ordering anything off the telly. Unless it's that appetite-suppressing lip gloss...

I put my dress back on the bed and walk over to the hall table where the box wrapped in brown paper and twine is sitting. The label has my name on it, but it gives no indication of who it's from.

I unwrap the parcel to discover it is a shoe box. When I open the lid I see the beautiful cream shoes from the store window inside with a small piece of white paper sitting on top.

To the girl who is beautiful from the inside out.

It has no signature, but my eyes smart with tears. I know who it is from.

I carry them over to the couch and run my fingers over the subtle giraffe spots and I wipe the tear that has slipped from my lashes.

I manage to get into my dress and shoes without any more tears. On the way to the Gala my hands are clutching the note from Oliver, and when I finally arrive I put it inside my clutch before making my way up the steps to the entrance of the tall glass building.

As I look around the room I can't believe how many people are here. It seems all of Makka's employees have attended, though looking around at the different faces I realise that I don't recognize half the people here.

They must be everyone's date-

Oh, God. I forgot about Nick!

I turn around and desperately search the entrance hall but know that I would have seen him if I had passed him. He agreed to meet me in the entrance at five-thirty, and when I look at my watch I see it's already quarter past six. My heart sinks at the realisation that he must have waited and then decided to go home.

When I asked Nick what he was doing tonight he told me he had a class. I proceeded to practically beg him to skip it and take me to the Gala instead... I even might have offered him a bribe.

He had laughed at what must have appeared utter desperation and asked why I couldn't come alone. After I had explained about Oliver and Angelica– though I referred to her as the snotty nosed bitch– he looked appalled. At first I thought it might have been my description of her, but afterwards he told me it was because he knew someone just like that, except male.

His boyfriend and he had started dating a while

ago, but recently his boyfriend has been seeing a friend that was trying to kick Nick out the picture.

"And if he thinks he can take my man–"

"Oh, so you're..." I cleared my throat, "gay then?"

In the end I convinced him that it would drive his boyfriend wild with jealousy if he thought he was going on a date tonight. Obviously he would have to insinuate that I was male– which usually I would be slightly offended at, but given the circumstances...

I look around the hall and note Malcolm and the other marketing people over in the corner with their wives. Malcolm's wife is wearing a black sequined gown with stilettos that have to be at least six inches tall. She is clinging onto Malcolm's arm and stroking it, though I have a suspicion it's more for balance than anything.

At the opposite end of the hall is a long table with shoes running along it. Towards the end I stop to admire a beautiful pair of red glitter shoes and like Dorothy I sigh and wish I could go home. "That's one of my favourites, too." I turn to see Anthony standing next to me while he runs his hand over the material.

"Are you having a nice time?" I ask as we continue to look at the shoes together.

"I guess." Anthony shrugs and takes two glasses

of champagne from the waiter standing behind him. "Though they're a bit tight with the bubbly aren't they?" He indicates the half full glass in his hand and passes me one.

I take a sip and look down at the next shoe.

"Hey," I point out, "you put the buckle on."

At the end of the final table is the shoe that Anthony let me try on. At the rim where the houndstooth material meets the leather Anthony has added a little hot pink buckle.

"Yes, well I thought it looked good," Anthony shrugs.

"Natalie, you made it." I turn to see Angelica and Oliver standing just behind me at the table. Angelica is wearing a burnt orange gown with feathers all over the bottom half of her mermaid style dress. The sweetheart neckline is barely containing her chest and it threatens to jump ship.

"Well, of course I–"

"Only, I was getting worried." Angelica checks the diamond encrusted watch on her wrist. "You didn't get lost, did you?" Angelica laughs.

"No, I didn't." I take another sip of champagne and see Anthony discreetly sneak away. Bastard.

"Oliver, have you seen the new final design for the Fall Line?" Angelica points to the shoe with the buckle. "Isn't it just divine? And I love the little details Anthony has added."

I open my mouth to tell her that I was the one who suggested the buckle, but close it. She'd never believe me anyways.

"So," Angelica's eyes look around and then settle back on my face, "where's your mysterious date?"

I hadn't made eye contact with Oliver yet, but at Angelica's words our eyes meet. I quickly look away when I see his eyes searching mine. He looks handsome as always, but in his suit and bowtie he could pass for a James Bond character. His rich blue eyes are intensified with the blackness of his jacket and the offset of his crisp white shirt.

"Oh, he's around," I gesture to the room but my voice shakes slightly.

Angelica seems to catch my hesitation and continues. "Well, we'd love to meet him. Wouldn't we Olly?" Angelica clings to Oliver's arm and it takes all my strength not to wretch her hands free.

"Are you going to introduce us?" Angelica searches the room for my date, but I can tell she thinks I haven't got one. "I'm dying to see– I mean, meet him." Angelica corrects herself with a laugh.

"Angelica," Oliver says in a warning tone.

Angelica ignores him and steps closer to me.

"He is here, right Natalie?"

"I–" I look from Angelica to Oliver and I can

see that he is also wondering if I have a date, though his face has forced restraint etched on it.

"Well?" Angelica prompts.

"He's—" I look around wildly and my hands begin to shake. I try and think of something to say, something to stall for time, but nothing comes to my head. "He's—"

"There you are." I hear from behind me as I feel an arm wrap around my body. "I was beginning to think I had lost you." I turn my face to see Nick smiling down at me.

The relief floods through my body and I feel limp. Nick squeezes my waist for encouragement but turns to face Angelica.

"You must be Angelica," Nick shakes her hand with his free arm. "I've heard quite a lot about you."

Angelica seems stunned that Nick actually exists, but recovers quickly with a light laugh. "All good, I hope."

"Oh— er— sure." Nick smiles and the laugh falters on her face.

"And you must be Oliver." Nick shakes his hand. "Nice to meet you."

"Yes, nice to meet you too." He looks from Nick to me. "You're a very lucky man."

I look into Oliver's eyes and see a sense of agony in his features. His gaze takes in my appearance, almost memorizing my face, and sadness washes over me.

"Don't I know it." Nick laughs and I feel the weight of his arm around me.

I'm still gazing at Oliver and the hurt I can see and suddenly I wish that Nick had never showed up to rescue me. Maybe I should have given Oliver the benefit of the doubt. Maybe I was asking too much of him too soon. I know he made mistakes, but I can't help but feel that in this moment I've made more.

"Oliver, isn't it time for your speech?" Angelica asks and she strokes his arm.

"Yes, I suppose it is." He nods to Nick and looks at me one more time before heading off in the direction of the stage. Angelica is still clinging to his arm, though Oliver seems oblivious to her attachment.

"Bloody hell, where have you been?" Nick asks.

"I'm so sorry," I apologize and take my attention off of Oliver's distancing back. "I was late getting home."

"It's alright," Nick sighs and then gives a wide grin. "I've actually been having a pretty good time. There are lots of cute prospects here."

I nod absently and take another sip of my champagne.

"So that's the guy you're madly in love with?" Nick nods his head towards Oliver.

"I'm not madly in love with him!" I deny, but lower my voice when I notice some heads turn in our direction. "I just liked him. But it doesn't matter, I'm not sure if he is interested," I sigh.

"Honey, if that guy isn't interested, then I don't have a tattoo of Cher on my ass."

"You have a tattoo of Cher?" I laugh incredulously and can't help but sneak a peek at his tuxedo clad bottom. "You should talk to Hank, he loves her."

"Which one's Hank, then?" Nick peers over the crowd.

"He's the one with the thick glasses," I point to the corner where Hank is standing with Rachel. "But he's not gay, at least, not yet anyways."

Nick smiles when he sees Hank. "Any man that wears a brown suede suit is either gay, or a cowboy." Nick raises his eyebrows. "Or hopefully both."

Oliver stands on the stage and looks like he was born to be there, and everyone stops chatting to look at him. He doesn't look nervous at all under the spotlight or in front of all the strangers. Seeing him like this, on stage with everyone looking up at him, I suddenly understand why he so desperately clings onto the man he's made himself into. He looks like he was born to be up there, with the crowd waiting on his every word; I see why he wouldn't want to lose that, and I question why he thinks he would have to.

"Ladies and Gentleman. Thank you for attending the unveiling of Makka's new Fall Collection. Obviously this is not just another new line. Makka has undergone some changes recently, and I am here tonight to tell you about the new vision for its future."

"Makka is a company that was at a crossroads. Although they continue to design the finest in women's shoes. they were looking for a new direction for their company. As I stand before you today I feel confident in the fact that they are quickly on their way to achieving this goal."

"And with that," Oliver steps to the side and watches as the lights turn off and a video begins on the far wall.

I'm mesmerized by the images that are flashing before me. They're some of the most beautiful shoes I've ever seen. One is a soft cream colour with rhinestone embedded in the fabric. Another flash and a teal sling back with tiny white polka dots is displayed. I hear the oohs and aahs from the crowd as the images disappear and are replaced with new ones.

"We have been inspired to join together and create a new line of shoes, one that will put Makka ahead of its competitors and something we can truly be proud of. We are going for subtle simple lines that people will stop and be mesmerized by."

"We're stepping away from the obvious and into something only the worthy will notice," Oliver says as more shoes flash behind him.

I smile at Oliver's words, but something is niggling at the back of my mind.

"No more bending to the demands of others," Oliver says and points to a shoe on the screen. "We are going to be unique– one of a kind."

I nod my head– that's a good selling feature, though for some reason it seems... *familiar.*

"We want women who are not willing to compromise to wear our shoes." Oliver continues, "women who have been let down by other brands, in style and comfort."

I– wait a minute.

"Ladies and Gentlemen I give you Makka's new line: Ten. For the woman who is beautiful from the inside out."

That bastard.

The whole room seems to slow down as the applause rings out. I stand frozen in place with my eyes glued to Oliver. He places the microphone back on the stand and steps off the stage.

Those were my ideas, *my words*, I feel like yelling. I look to the table and see the shoe with the hot pink buckle and have to hold back the tears.

He betrayed me. I thought he was my friend; I thought he liked me and he was confused. All this time he was just using me. That's why he didn't tell Angelica to bugger off. He wasn't interested in me, he was just interested in my ideas.

As I look back at the stage my hurt turns to rage, and my eyes seek Oliver out in the crowd. I hand Nick my glass of champagne and begin to make my way to the other side of the room.

I could go home. I could cry and just add Oliver to the list of bastards that have screwed me over– but then what? All I'm left with is another sob story to tell. Well, I already have too many of those, and I don't fancy another one.

To The Man of My Dreams,

To cut a long story short, I've been had. Betrayed. Blind-sided. I shall never trust another human being in my entire life (except my therapist– if I can ever afford one that is– but only because I am paying them to keep my secrets. At least then I have a money back guarantee.).

Hope to be seeing you soon,

Natalie Flemming

P.S. Do you have a decent therapist that you could recommend? Maybe we could get a group discount rate.

Thirteen

"You bastard!"

Oliver and Angelica are standing in a group with champagne in their hands, and I think they were just about to toast to something.

Okay, on second thought, maybe I should have asked for a word in private.

"Excuse me?" an executive says while looking around at the other people in the group.

"Not you– him." I point to Oliver but feel slightly less confident than when I came up with this plan.

See, that's the problem with on the fly decisions. They're so much fun to watch other people carry out, but when it's yourself, you wish you had thought it through a bit more.

"Natalie, would you like a word?" Oliver hands his glass to Angelica and takes hold of my elbow. "Excuse us, please."

As I'm led away by Oliver I feel like a huge prat, but when I think of the reasons why I was going to confront him in the first place, my resolve returns.

I take back my elbow and gesture Oliver to the exit door, leading to what I assume is a stairwell. Once we are inside the corridor I turn to face him, but now that we're alone I'm at a loss for words.

"Listen Natalie," Oliver approaches me, "I want to explain–"

"No." I cross my arms over my chest.

"No?"

"I think you've said enough already, and now it's my turn." I walk past him to the railing and then turn to face him again. "When I told you those things, those very personal things, I didn't want you to use them as your next project."

I look at my hands and then look back at him, my eyes brimming with tears. "I trusted you and you used me."

"Natalie," Oliver begins to approach me and stops, "I didn't mean to betray your trust. They were great ideas and they were true–"

"Yes, but they weren't your ideas!" I throw my arms up in the air.

"I know you think I betrayed you, but–"

"It's not about you betraying me– though I think you're a complete ass for it." I run my hands through my hair and it gets stuck in the curls. I yank it free and continue, "They were my ideas and you stole them. I was creative and you got the credit."

"But, Natalie–" Oliver is trying to stop me, but I can't let him. I have to get this off my chest.

"Can't you see what you have become? You were so angry when Spencer did this to me, but for you it's okay? Anything to get you a little bit more success, right?"

"If you would just let me explain–"

"Explain *what* exactly? That you were using me this whole time? That you made me believe that you really cared about me when all you were doing was picking my brains for your stupid marketing campaign?" I shake my head. "I told you all those ridiculous ideas and you just told me to keep at it, but never once did you tell me I might be on to something because you just wanted all the glory for yourself."

There, I said it. I trusted him. I was falling in love with him. I thought he felt the same way, but he was never interested in me like that.

I can't stop the tears from rolling down, and I lean on the railing for support. I feel Oliver's hands on my arms but I try and shrug off his embrace.

"Don't," I whisper.

"Natalie, I was going to tell the executives tomorrow at the board meeting that I think you should head up this new marketing division." Oliver's deep voice comes from behind me. "It's all in my report- how these ideas were yours and that you should be rewarded for it."

"What?" I heard him, but I'm not sure I *really* heard him. "But, your speech–" I turn around to search his face.

"I said I was inspired." He takes his hand and tucks a loose curl behind my ear. "I made sure the report is clear you were the inspiration."

I don't know what to say. I always have something to say, even if it's bollocks, but I am speechless.

I'm the inspiration.

I'm going to be the new marketing lead.

"But, I don't understand. Why didn't you just tell me all of this weeks ago? Why did you need to keep me in the dark?"

"I wanted to tell you, I even tried to tell you that day you spilled juice all over your trousers. Then you came into my office and you told me you were bringing a date to this thing– well, quite frankly, I was too mad to talk to you about anything at that point."

"This doesn't make sense, you have had weeks to tell me," I argue.

Oliver rubs his hand over the back of his neck and I can tell he is looking for the right words to say. "Maybe I should have told you, but every time I kept pushing you to come up with ideas they were..."

"Crap," I supply.

"I was going to say they needed some more work," he says in a placating tone.

I give him a stern look and he nods and holds up his hands in defense.

"Alright, they were crap. The point is, when you *tried* nothing was working, but when you just relaxed and spoke from your heart you were saying some of the most insightful things I have ever heard." He looks down and shakes his head before returning my gaze. "I thought if you could see what you are capable of, if you could just let go of your constant need to prove yourself to everyone, then you might see how brilliant you really are."

"Oliver, I–"

"I know what I did was inexcusable," he looks at the door, then back in my eyes, "but Natalie, you're special. You know things. You know things that everyone knows but no one else *notices*. But, you just can't admit what you're capable of. I know I broke your trust, but if it was the only way for you to put yourself out there, then I'm not sorry."

Oliver frowns at his own words. I can tell he is waiting for me to say something, but my brain is having a hard time processing everything.

He thinks I'm special.

Oliver runs his hand through his hair and looks

at the ground.

"I'm sorry I hurt you– if you believe nothing else, please believe that was something I never wanted to do."

Nothing has changed. I know that, but looking at Oliver and listening to his words, I'm not worried anymore. I know he can't promise me forever, but who can? I always want to see things in black and white but the whole world is grey. There are no certainties.

He turns and starts walking down the stairs, and as I watch him disappear round the corner my brain finally kicks into action.

"Oliver– wait!" I start running down the stairs but my shoes get the better of me. I'm just a few steps up from Oliver, he turns just as my toe catches on the hem of my dress and I go flying forwards, crashing into his arms.

He steadies me but doesn't let me out of his grasp. Instead he pushes the hair back from my face with a concerned look.

"Natalie, are you alright?"

Abandoning my doubts and forgetting about the consequences, I kiss him with such force it throws me slightly off balance again. Oliver wraps his arms around me and steals my breath with his passion and need. As my body arches toward him I put my hands on his warm chest and slowly raise them until they are wrapped around his neck, clinging on for balance, but more importantly from a desire to hold on and never let go. The sound from the party is still flowing through the stairwell and I can hear laughter from the guests. The noise forces me to break the kiss and ask Oliver something I desperately need to know.

"Oliver, what about Angelica?" I argue.

"There will never be anything between Angelica and myself, and she knows it," Oliver argues. "She works for me, that's it."

I nod, but I know despite what Oliver thinks Angelica won't ever stop pursuing him.

"Natalie, about what I said the other day–"

I raise my hand to his lips and shake my head. "Don't. We don't know what's going to happen tomorrow or the day after that. Is it wrong for us to just enjoy whatever time we have together while we have it?"

I realise I am asking this as much of myself as I am Oliver.

"I know you, I know all the things that you want," he argues.

"Right now, I just want you. For however long I can have you."

I bite my bottom lip to try and contain the smile

that is overflowing from inside of me, which causes Oliver's eyes to darken and to pull me closer. I lean my face towards his, seeking his mouth, but he places his fingertips on my lips to stop me. "I think you should come back to my place," he adds, "so I can show you that report."

I smile and look at him from under my lashes. "I suppose that would be the proper thing to do– my name being mentioned and all."

Oliver runs his thumb over the pulse on my neck which makes me extremely hot and bothered, then he takes my hand and we walk down the stairs.

"Wait–" He stops and my heart plunges at the thought he might have changed his mind. "What about Nick?"

"Nick?" I ask puzzled.

Oliver raises his eyebrows. "Your date."

"Oh, *Nick.*" I nod. "Not to worry, he's gay and probably hitting on Hank right now."

Oliver looks confused but I tug on his hand.

"Don't worry, I'll explain later."

We go back to Oliver's place and he hands me his proposal.

He shows me all the lovely things he wrote about me over a nice glass of champagne. There's one part that I suggest needs a little bit of work.

"I don't see anywhere in this proposal that says how charming and beautiful I am." I shake my head in mock disapproval. "I think the executives definitely need to know that."

"It doesn't?" Oliver frowns and leans over me to get a better look at the paperwork, "I could have sworn I put that in here somewhere."

He takes the papers and starts scanning them with his eyes. "Ahh, here we are," he says, pointing to a section on the third page in. "The brain behind this new marketing venture is both charming and beautiful with a keen eye for detail."

I grab the piece of paper back from him and look at where he pointed. Of course it doesn't actually say that, but I thought I should check– just in case.

After another glass of champagne we sit by the fire with Oliver's arms wrapped around me so I am snuggled under his chin, and we stare at the flames in silence.

I've never felt so content to be sitting with someone and not saying a word. Before this, silence has always felt lonely. But, with Oliver, it isn't. With Oliver, silence is peaceful.

He slowly trails kisses along my cheek bone and sends jolts of electricity to the pit of my stomach. I've never felt so connected to someone in my life, and every part of me wants more of Oliver. When our mouths finally meet the passion in his touch overwhelms me and the whole room seems to spin around us. He reaches behind me to the zipper on my dress and I start to unbutton the front of his shirt to reveal hard muscle and smooth skin. My cold hands on his chest cause a low groan from his throat and I shiver from anticipation.

"Natalie," Oliver pulls his head back slightly to look into my eyes, "I want to make sure you're not going to regret this–"

I place my finger over his mouth. "Has anyone ever told you that you think too much?" I tease. "We'll just take it one step at a time."

Oliver narrows his eyes and opens his mouth to say more, but I silence him with another kiss and pull him on top of me as I slowly lean backwards onto the floor.

We spend the better part of the evening in front of the fire, and then move into the bedroom where I even attempt a fancy move from one of Hank's books, but I end up falling over the footboard in my efforts.

Now, I'm not going to give you any specifics; after all, a girl has to have her modesty. I will say, though, besides the minor incident– which I think I might have a slight concussion from– it was sensational.

"You know, this is going to be a lot of extra work for you," Oliver says as he starts buttoning up his shirt the next morning. "You may have to come in early, stay late..." He starts to give me a slow smile. "It's lucky you don't have some crazy, non-understanding boyfriend around."

Oh God, I would definitely call this a good sign. Usually it's so awkward after– well, you know– but Oliver is being so nice.

I think–

I mean, I'm pretty sure–

I think we might be starting something here. Something very special. Hank's right, he definitely *like* likes me.

"Well, I guess I'll just have to find someone who can appreciate having a successful girlfriend." I smile.

Who is this woman? I sound so cool, so *not* me. I don't know why but the right things always seem to come out of my mouth whenever he's around. I don't have to think about the right thing to say, I just say it.

I finish zipping up my dress. "I better go home and get ready for work," I say.

"Yes, big day for you today." Oliver keeps kissing me as we walk to the door and I'm not sure I am going to have the strength to leave. "You'll probably need to put together a team of people... they'll have to be willing to work overtime to get things going, considering the deadline."

After I finally manage to get his hand off my zipper he begrudgingly settles for a quick kiss and picks up his briefcase before he opens the door. "Do you know of anyone?"

"You know," I smile, "I already know one person perfect for the job."

~

Rachel bursts into tears when I ask her to help me with the new marketing team. I tell her it isn't official yet, but when I mention all the overtime we will have to do she promises me her left kidney should I ever need it.

I saw Oliver go into the board meeting an hour ago. I sheepishly grinned at him when he winked at me and have been on cloud nine since then.

"So?" Hank taps his foot beside my desk.

"So, what?" I reply as I study a paystub from last month.

"Did you sleep with him?" Hank sighs and sits on my desk. "We all saw you leaving together. Angelica was pissed, to say the least."

I open my eyes wide and try and think of

something to say without giving myself away. "I can't tell you that. It's private."

"They slept together," Hank tells Rachel knowingly.

I open my mouth to object but my face goes bright red, and I can't help the wide smile that comes over my face.

"So, what now?" Rachel worriedly looks at me.

"What do you mean, what now?" I question.

"Well, are you guys going to continue to see each other once he leaves?"

"I– er..." I look from Hank to Rachel, "I'm not entirely sure to be honest, we didn't discuss it."

"Well, don't you think you should?" Hank argues.

"I can't bring it up. We've only spent one night together." And Oliver's a little new to this long-term relationship business, so bringing up the future after one night together might send him bolting in the opposite direction. "He'll think I'm all clingy."

"You're going to have to," Rachel comes to sit beside me. "You and Oliver seem to have a really strong connection, don't you want to pursue it?"

Of course I want to pursue it. Oliver is the most wonderful man I have ever met, and I am pretty sure I love him (though I would never admit as much to Hank and Rachel). But, I don't want to scare him off. We have time before he leaves.

Well, a week...

Hank must have seen the panicked look on my face and he gently pats my hand.

"Maybe he is waiting for you to bring it up," Hank looks to Rachel for encouragement.

"Have you shown him that you want to pursue the relationship after he leaves?" Rachel asks.

I try to quickly search my brain. "Well, he knows how much I care about him, so I'm sure he knows how I feel. I've dropped some not-so-subtle hints."

"No," Hank shakes his head in frustration. "Men don't get things from hints or clues. You have to *tell* him."

"I can't!"

"It's okay, you can do this," Hank says encouragingly.

"No, really, I can't," I argue. "Every time I have ever told a guy how I feel about him I could tell straight off I scared the pants off him, and then it becomes so awkward."

"Oh! I know what to do." Rachel claps her hands. "You can email him."

"Email him what?" I frown.

"How you feel." Rachel says, as though it's the obvious solution.

"No, I can't," I argue. "Then I will be walking

on eggshells until I see him."

"Well," Hank reasons, "you have to tell him one way or the other. So you either tell him to his face, or you can email him."

"Ughh." I lower my head to my desk and shake my head.

"It will be fine." Rachel pats me on the back, and Hank presses some buttons on my computer.

"There," he says with a final click. "It's all ready to go."

I look up to see my email browser on the screen and Hank has filled in the top section.

To: Oliver Miles (olivermiles@westcottsolutions.co.uk)
From: Natalie Flemming (nflemming@makka.co.uk)
Subject: My Unwavering Declaration of Love

"Hank!" I yell and quickly grab the mouse from his hand. "I am not putting that as the subject."

"Fine, do it your way," he shrugs.

"Come on, Hank." Rachel takes his arm and pulls him to the door. "Let's get a cup of coffee and leave Natalie to it."

I watch Rachel drag Hank down the corridor before returning to my computer screen.

They're right, Oliver is leaving soon and he needs to know how I feel. I know what he said about the future, and I know I told him that I wouldn't pressure him into anything, but that was before we spent the night together. I mean, that changes things, doesn't it?

You know, it probably wouldn't be a bad idea just to write the email. I mean, I won't send it to him, but at least I can practise what I *would* say.

Dear Oliver,

It's me. Natalie Flemming. Your little love tigress (note to self: take this out when actually speaking to Oliver). I know we just started seeing each other; last night was the first night we ever... well you know... and you are probably going to think I am mental for even having this conversation with you so soon.

The thing is though, and I am not sure really how to say this other than to just say it, I think I am in love with you. Actually, I know I am in love with you.

You know things about me, you know things that everyone knows but no one takes the time to notice. Before you came along I had to search the want ads to find the man of my dreams. Not because no one would go out with me, but because no one wanted to take the time to get to know the real me. They were satisfied to just see what they wanted to see, and I always went along with it because I was too afraid that the real me just wasn't good enough.

I know your company is important to you, and I would never want you to give that up for me. I just want you to allow yourself to be happy in all aspects of your life.

You see me, you see all of me and want to be with me because of that. And I wanted you to know before you have to leave with that bitch Angelica (note to self: try not to be too jealous and possessive when having the real conversation with Oliver) that I love all of you.

So there it is, my undying declaration of love to the man of my dreams.

Natalie.

I press the save button and sit back with a feeling of peace. I did it, I found the man of my dreams and now I just have to find the courage to tell him.

My hands start to shake at the prospect and I decide to go and get some coffee. When I walk to the coffee machine I can see everyone still in the board meeting, and I sigh when I try to pour a cup of coffee and the pot is empty.

I have time to run to the coffee shop before the meeting finishes, so I go back to the office to grab my jacket and purse and rush out and down the steps to the shop around the corner.

I get a coffee for Hank and Rachel while I'm there and decide to pick one up for Oliver as well. I mean, not that I am trying to butter him up or anything. Okay, so I just happened to get him a slice of his favourite cake– but it's only because I am a nice person. Obviously he wouldn't say he loved me back just because of the cake.

Though, I'm not saying it won't help.

After paying the lady behind the counter I make my way back to Makka, running the words over and over again in my head. I get on the lift and notice that George from Fabrication is on as well so I smile and wave, but he just nods and avoids my eyes, though I think I can see a smile on his lips. As the lift doors open at our floor he quickly gets out and starts laughing while walking away.

What is his problem?

As I'm walking through Reception things begin to get even weirder.

"Natalie!" Claire stands up from behind her desk and beams at me. I think it is the first time she has actually acknowledged my presence unless she was tattling on me for something, but I can't think of anything I have done. "So sorry to hear things haven't been going well for you lately." Claire giggles and looks over at Margaret from Marketing.

"Er– things are fine." I frown in confusion and

walk towards my office.

"Natalie," Anthony walks up to me and winks. "I just knew you would be a feisty one. Roar."

"Umm... okay?" I look around in confusion.

I frown as he walks away and quickly race back to my office. I can hear laughter and whispering behind me, and when I get inside I quickly close the door.

"Okay, what the hell is going on?" I ask Rachel and Hank, who both look nervous and worried. "Everyone is acting really weird."

"I think you better sit down." Hank pulls out a chair.

"I don't need to sit down." I place the coffee on my desk and start unbuttoning my jacket.

"Trust me," Hank nods, "you do."

I give him a very wary look and carefully sit down.

"Well, what is it?"

I always get very nervous when people don't tell me things, my mind always jumps to the worst case scenario. Like, maybe I have my skirt tucked into my underwear and everyone can see my blue polka dot thong.

"Umm... well... just keep in mind that it's not a big deal," Rachel reassures me. "No one will–"

"Just tell me," I interrupt.

"You cocked up your email somehow and sent it to everyone," Hank says.

"I– what email?" I get up from the chair but panic is starting to take over.

"That one you wrote to Oliver." Rachel starts to bite on her fingernail.

My hands shake as I look widely around the room. I focus in on my computer and quickly open up my email browser. When I click on sent messages I see it is the first one on the list. When I click 'TO' the message reads 'MAKKA COMPANY LIST: SENT ALL'.

Oh.

Sweet.

Jesus.

How the bloody hell did I do that? I don't even know how to send out a massive email like that if I tried, and the computer did it all on its own!

"Oh God," I cry and collapse in my chair.

Hank comes to my desk and shrugs. "I don't know what the big deal is. Everyone knows you and Oliver have a thing... and so you've been searching the want ads; that's how I found my flat for five hundred quid a month."

"Yes, Hank," I point out, "but you weren't searching for a man, were you? You were searching for a bloody kitchen and bathroom."

I pick up my jacket and bag and run out of my office, and as I pass the boardroom my heart sinks even further.

Oliver will know. He will have seen the email on his phone and know what I did. He'll know he just slept with someone and she has gone and declared it to the entire world! If he was scared of commitment before, I can guarantee he will be terrified of it by the end of the day.

I run to the tube as fast as I can and silently cry the whole way home. This is so much worse than my worst case scenario. I would *love* to have my skirt tucked into my knickers.

I finally had things sorted. I had a great guy, a great job, and great friends, and then I had to go and send out a bloody email declaring to the world– well, to everyone I work with, which if you think about it, is a bloody big part of my world– my undying love of a man I only slept with yesterday!

When I reach my flat, I open the door and walk over to the phone to yank the cord from the wall. Running into my bedroom, I throw myself face down on my bed.

The next morning the phone is still unplugged and no one has come by the flat. I vaguely feel like I should call into work, but then the mere thought that everyone knows and is laughing at me puts me right back into my stupor.

I knew how Oliver felt. I knew he couldn't promise me forever, but I pushed for it anyways. I wanted to be the girl that every woman aspires to be– the girl who can change a man.

I should probably run away, it's the only sensible solution. My job is crap, my love life is in ruins and I'm all alone, yet again. I might as well commit to being a cat lady for the rest of my life.

Actually, I'm allergic to cats and I'm not very good with remembering to feed things. I'll have to be a fish lady– at least they have those special tanks now that do all the work.

But, as I sit here thinking of a clever name for my new goldfish, I realise that it doesn't matter what I buy for myself; it's not going to make this all better. I don't want to be alone anymore. That's why I put that want ad in Lasso. I didn't want to be alone.

On the end table beside me I see a picture of me smiling at my friend's wedding last summer. It was so hot that day that the bride needed constant fanning to cool down (unfortunately I was given the task, which meant I was sweating by the end of the night). Right after this picture was taken they were ready to cut the cake, but the bride and groom had run off somewhere. When I went to go and find them they were in the garden, slowly dancing under a tree with their arms wrapped around each other. I stood there, in awe, watching them, and a sadness and longing took over me that was so painful I thought I might suffocate. I hadn't realised what I was missing until I saw it right in front of me. I placed the want ad the next week.

It didn't go according to plan– actually, it went in the complete opposite direction of what I had planned. But even sitting here with a broken heart and runny mascara, I don't regret it.

Things aren't really at their best right now, but as gloomy as things look, I honestly believe I am closer to finding love than I was. Any step, no matter how small, is one step closer. I thought I was giving fate a break by taking things into my own hands, but fate was here the whole time.

I'm dreading going to work tomorrow. But, it's one more step towards my happily ever after.

And I'd walk over hot coals any day for the man of my dreams.

To The Man of My Dreams,

I thought I had it all sorted. I thought I found you, but I messed everything up before it even had a chance to begin. I'm not sure what to do anymore.

I do know one thing, though. I will never touch another computer again. Which, as you may know from my love of online shopping, is quite a sacrifice for me. But, I cannot afford another disaster in my life. What happens if the computer cocks up again and I buy ten pairs of trousers by accident?

Hope to be seeing you soon,

Natalie Flemming.

P.S. I would like to tell you that is what happened if you happen to see my online shopping bill next month, but it would be unfair to lie about it to you. My account was hacked by a cunning thief who happened to buy the same things that I already had in my wardrobe from ages ago. These internet thieves are so tricky now a days...

Fourteen

Having made the decision to go to work, but still wary, I figure there is no harm in getting out of bed and just making the commute to Makka. If I don't feel like going in when I get there, well, at least I got out of the flat for a bit.

I shower and blow-dry my hair and take my time picking out an outfit and putting it on.

The familiarity of the commute to Makka makes me feel better, but I stop on the sidewalk across the street and stare at the building. I'm unsure if I'm willing to take the final steps and walk through the door. I stand, stranded on the sidewalk, thinking about all the things I have done in the past couple of months and can't help but smile. Looking back it was terrifying to be so far out of the bubble I had forced myself to live in, and I can honestly say it was the best time I've ever had.

Okay, I sent out an email telling everyone how much I love Oliver. So what– it's true. Am I supposed to hide away forever and be miserable?

Even Ghandi said "Freedom is not worth having

if it does not include the freedom to make mistakes". Now, I'm not sure he was referring to *exactly* the same situation as mine– I'm not sure if he even knew what email is– but I'm sure he wanted it to be universally applied.

I walk across the street and hold my head up high as I walk into the building. I can do this.

The lift is empty when the doors open and as I get inside and press the button for my floor, I feel slightly disappointed. I was hoping I would bump into someone from Makka on the way up so I could gage their reaction to my being back at work. Not that I care, just so I would have a better idea of what I'm about to face. At least, that's what I am telling myself.

The lift finally beeps and the doors open to reveal Makka's main reception. Claire is at her desk and typing something on the computer. I slowly walk by her desk and try not to draw attention to myself.

"Why are you doing that?" Claire asks, and I jump at the sound of her voice.

"Doing what?" I look around to see if people are watching or pointing and laughing.

"Walking on your toes and looking at the ceiling." Claire looks at me as though I've lost my mind.

"Oh, I... I was just checking for any

watermarks," I point to the ceiling.

"So weird," I hear her mutter as she starts typing again.

I cautiously continue past Claire's desk and down the corridor to my office. I stop in my tracks, though, when I turn the corner and see Anthony and Carl by the coffee maker. I look in all directions to see if there is another way to get to my office, but I know there isn't. Taking a deep breath, I raise my chin in the air and make the long walk down the hall.

Anthony and Carl are busy chatting with each other and as I quickly try to sneak by– practically plastering my body against the wall so as to not draw attention to myself– Anthony spots me.

He gives me a wide grin and puts down his coffee. "Just the girl I was after."

I sigh as he speaks and square my shoulders to face them, ready to receive their ridicule.

"What do you want?" I look down my nose at them and fold my arms across my chest.

"I need you to try on a pair of shoes for me and see what you think," Anthony says, though I can see he is hesitating by the way I'm looking at him.

"Why?" I accuse, "because no one else's fat foot will fit in them?"

"Er– no," Anthony looks at Carl in confusion, "because I know you will tell me if they are good or not."

"Oh, I–" I'm shocked at Anthony's response but try and recover quickly, "sure. Okay."

"Alright," Anthony is still giving me a reserved look and quickly picks up his coffee and nudges Carl. "We'll be in the studio whenever you have time."

I nod as they leave, but don't turn my back to them– just in case they plan to hurl insults at me when it's turned. As they round the corner I begin to relax.

I cautiously continue down the hall until I reach my office, open the door and slowly close it once I'm inside. Only Rachel is there, typing away at her computer.

"Er– Hi Rachel." I put my bag down by my desk and start to peel off my coat.

"Oh, hi Natalie." Rachel continues typing as though it is any other day at work.

"So," I frown and look around the office, "how are things?"

"Fine," Rachel shrugs and points to my desk, "your mail is in you in-tray."

I pick up the mail and leaf through it, though I can't focus on what any of it says.

"So," I say casually as I stare at Rachel, watching for her reaction, "where's Hank?"

"He's not in yet, I don't think," Rachel shrugs

but continues typing. "At least, I didn't see him this morning-"

"What the hell is going on here?" I yell and throw my hands in the air, spraying my mail everywhere.

Rachel looks up, startled.

"What do you mean?"

"I mean, two days ago I was run out of here by laughter and finger pointing, and today no one seems to even remember it happened."

Rachel looks like she is trying to think about what I am talking about when her eyes open in sudden realisation.

"Oh," she nods, "you mean about your *email*?"

"Yes, of course the email!" I walk over to her desk. "Unless there is another extremely embarrassing thing I did that I have no recollection of."

Rachel waves her hand away and smiles. "That's old news."

"Old news?" I ask, and for some reason feel slightly offended. "It happened two days ago."

"Yes," Rachel smiles and leans forward, "but *yesterday* Hank came out the closet."

I gasp and put my hand to my face. "NO!"

"Yes." Rachel seems thrilled to meet someone that doesn't know the news, and she quickly begins to tell me all the details. "He met a guy at the Gala and they started talking. Well, I suppose one thing led to another and he walked in here first thing yesterday morning and announced to anyone who would listen that he was as gay as it gets!"

"NO!" I repeat in shock.

"Yes, so," Rachel points out, "as you can see your email was quickly forgotten."

"I can't believe I missed that!"

"Good morning my lovely little straight friends," Hank comes through the door and walks over to the coat stand. He takes off his bright white coat with a fur collar to reveal a t-shirt that says: *GAY BY BIRTH. FABULOUS BY CHOICE.*

I smile as Hank skips over to my desk and sits down on the edge.

"So," I point to his shirt, "you have some news, I see."

"Natalie, you should hear this from me first." Hank takes hold of both of my hands. "I'm gay."

"I–"

"No, now I know what you're going to say, and don't think I haven't already heard it from my mother," Hank holds up his hand. "But, I've thought this through and I cannot deny it to myself any longer."

I get up out of my chair and give Hank a big

hug. "I'm very happy for you."

"Careful not to ruin my hair." He pats me on the back and I let go. He gently touches his head to make sure no hairs are out of place.

"So, what was the- er... inspiration?"

"I met a fabulous guy the other night," Hank beams from ear to ear, "and we just hit it off."

"Really?" I look at my friend smiling like the cat who swallowed the canary. "Do I know him?"

"As a matter of fact you do!" Hank leans forward. "It's Nick."

"Nick?" I shake my head and frown. "As in my date for the Gala? But he has a boyfriend," I point out.

"Not anymore." Hank gets up and walks over to his own desk. "Chucked him."

"Wow."

Who would have thought? Not that Hank is gay– I mean, I think we all thought that. But that I, Natalie Flemming, would be responsible for it. After all, I was the one who brought Nick to the Gala, and I was the one who pointed Hank out to him.

Maybe I could make a living off this... Natalie Flemming: Matchmaker and Realise-You're-Secretly-Gay Extraordinaire.

Hank starts sorting through the file cabinet looking for something while I sit and stare at my computer.

No one remembers. I spent all that time worrying about what everyone thought and they don't even remember. A part of me feels slightly offended that I could be so easily forgotten; then another part– a much, much, bigger part– is so relieved.

"What's this?" I ask as I spot an envelope bearing my name tucked against the printer.

"One of the executives dropped it off for you yesterday." Hank shrugs. "Probably a memo about using the executive's loo."

Dear Miss. Natalie Flemming,

We are pleased to offer you the position of Lead Marketing Director at Makka. Due to your current position there will be an overlap period for transition, but we do not see this being a problem. We would be delighted to meet with you this coming Monday at 3:30pm in the boardroom to discuss and to present you with your new contract if you should accept the position.

Regards.

I got the job. I got the job. The thought keeps repeating over and over again in my head, but I still can't believe it.

I got the job because I was creative. I got the

job because I am smart and talented. I got the job because of Oliver.

"Rachel, you– er– don't happen to know how I can get a hold of someone at Westcott Solutions, do you?"

"I'm sure you can just call their main line and be patched through," she reasons.

I nod and slump in my chair.

"Unless of course that person you are wishing to contact is Oliver," Rachel adds, "then you won't be able to reach him there."

I turn around. "Why's that?"

"He's taken some time off, I believe." Rachel smiles and continues typing.

"He's taking time off?" I step towards her desk. "But, why?"

"Rumour is he found something else that he wants to focus on." Rachel shares a smile with Hank before she picks up her glasses and puts them on.

The hope is bubbling inside me at what Rachel is implying. I know I've been down this road before, getting my hopes up only to have them crushed. But, I'm still here. I'm still standing. I know it's worth the risk. It's worth everything.

"Well, did he leave a phone number for me to reach him?"

She shrugs, "I'm not sure."

I feel slightly deflated at the news and turn to sit down again when she adds, "Though if you wanted to talk to him you could always just look down the hall."

My hand freezes on my chair.

"Down the hall?"

"Yes," Rachel picks up the file in front of her and starts reading something. "He's offered his personal services to us for a little while longer to help with the transition period. He still has his office in Marketing, I think."

He's here.

To The Man of My Dreams,

Hold on tight, I'm on my way.

Natalie Flemming

P.S. I'm thinking of starting a dating service as I seem to be extremely gifted and have wonderful success rates for my matchmaking abilities. I can't have a website though, as I've lost my trust in the internet.

Fifteen

I push the door open without another word to Rachel and Hank, dash down the hallway, and run through the doors of the Marketing Department. I weave through the cubicles and wave at some people as they say hello, trying get to Oliver's office.

"Oliver!" I throw open the door without knocking.

He's sitting at his desk, with piles of paper stacked around the room that are balancing precariously in place, and I have to smile. It's exactly how my office looked a few weeks ago.

He is in the middle of writing something on a post-it note, but when he sees me a look of surprise comes across his face.

"Natalie, where have you *been*?" He stands up and walks over to me. "I've tried calling... I went to your flat but your buzzer wasn't working..."

"Oliver I– you went to my flat?"

"Yes, I wanted to bring you those." He points to a small white plastic bag hanging on his coat rack.

I squint at the bag and turn back to Oliver. "Are

227

those lemons?"

"For medicinal purposes, I thought they would make you feel better. I couldn't figure out where you went after the board meeting, and Hank mentioned you weren't feeling well so I just thought..."

I want to cry right then and there but contain myself. He bought me lemons. For medicinal purposes.

"Listen Oliver," I interrupt. "I know there are some things you read about me that were a bit– er– *sudden.*" I take a deep breath. "But that's before we met... well actually, it started around the time we met..."

"Natalie, what are you–"

"No, let me finish." I take a deep breath. "In the stairwell you said I was special. Well the truth is, you're the special one. Before you came along I was someone that desperately wanted to be noticed but was constantly ignored. You gave me a chance," I clench my fists for courage, "and now, I'm asking you to give me another one."

Oliver just stands there in silence and looks extremely uncertain.

Oh God, he doesn't know if he can. That's why he isn't saying anything– he's creeped out that I sent a massive email to everyone declaring my love, and now he has the exact same look on his face that I was dreading– bewilderment.

I can feel the tears brimming at the back of my eyes. "Please just be honest with me," I take a deep breath, "I can handle it."

"Well, honestly," he sighs and scratches his forehead, "I have no idea what you're talking about."

"The email," I tell him. "I meant to send it to you, well, actually I didn't mean to send it to anyone, but it was meant for you, and then it somehow got sent to the whole bloody office."

"What email?" Oliver frowns. "I didn't get an email."

"But–" I say perplexed, "it went to the whole office."

"Well, I'm not on your office email list," Oliver points out.

Oh, right. I didn't think about that.

"When I couldn't get a hold of you after the meeting, I tried going to your flat but you weren't there either. I knew you wouldn't just disappear like that, so I thought–" he stops and looks at his hands.

"What?"

At his continued silence I persist. "Oliver?"

"I thought you had changed your mind about me. About us. I told you I wasn't willing to give you what you wanted, and you decided that it wasn't enough. To be honest, the thought petrified me."

At my stricken look he shakes his head. "No, you misunderstand. Not the commitment, the thought of losing you yet again when I just got you back. I don't know why, but from the second I met you it seemed like everything I had wanted in life, everything I had been working so hard for, was insignificant, and the thought was terrifying. I had to admit to myself that all this time I had spent building myself up had been a waste."

"No, Oliver," I say touching his arm and finding it so very important that he finally understand what I've been trying to say to him all along. "Your dreams are an important part of you, they have made you into the wonderful man you are today. I never wanted you to give up your life for me; I just wanted to be a part of it."

Our hands are drawn together and for once I am giving Oliver the support he needs, when I feel this whole time he has been trying to hold me up.

"So I guess you didn't hear everyone talking about the email?" I ask.

"I left right after the meeting. I had another meeting scheduled with Angelica to discuss her permanent relocation to our Russia office." Oliver smiles. "I've decided to take some time off. Relax a little. I've been told I'm a little tense."

"You did?" Alright, I know Rachel already told

me, but he has this satisfied look on his face and I would rather hear it from him.

"You were right, about everything." Oliver takes my hand and pulls me over to his desk. "The only thing keeping me tied to a desk everyday is myself. I've worked hard to make my company a success, but it's time I made other areas of my life a priority, too."

"You didn't throw in the towel, did you?" I say, a little worried he might have gone to the other extreme.

"No, I'll still be active in the company, just not *so* active. I don't think I've had a weekend off in years."

"Really?" I ask as he pulls me into his arms. "What are you going to do with all that spare time?"

He takes a second to think about it before running his eyes over my face.

"I happen to know a beautiful woman who has a very active imagination. I'm sure we can put our heads together and come up with something." Oliver searches my gaze and his eyes lock onto my lips. "That is, if she still wants it all."

"That's what every girl wants," I say with a catch in my voice, and I raise my hands to let them rest on Oliver's warm chest.

"I hope you know what you're getting yourself into," I tease. "I know you're new to this whole relationship thing, but I'm afraid it's not all fun and games.   It's going to take dedication, time, commitment..."

"Hmm, and I suppose you will let me know exactly how it's done?" he asks as he places kisses on my cheek bone.

"Mmm," my breath catches as I close my eyes at the sensation. "Well, as an extreme sports enthusiast I do know a thing or two about those things."

"Right, I forgot." Oliver switches his lips to the other cheek. "And your love of cheap wine and guys with mustaches."

I smile but have to lift Oliver's face so it's even with mine to ask him a very important question. "You are sure, right? I mean, you know me – are you sure you wouldn't want to try this with someone more…"

He puts his fingers on my lips to stop me. "Only with you. I love you Natalie. It was always meant to be you."

"I love you too," I whisper as he devours my lips with his kiss. Oliver trails kisses down my neck and I have to blink to regain my focus.

"So, you didn't read my email, then?" I have to ask one more time, just to be sure.

"No, but now I'm very curious what it was about. Though, Claire was giggling a lot when I came in this morning." He shakes his head. "I thought I would be relieved when I couldn't get a hold of you, but instead I was terrified. Terrified I'd lost you and wouldn't be able to convince you to give me another chance. I knew I'd only need one to make you mine forever."

"We were both afraid we lost each other."

I look down at his hand, weaved into mine, and decide it's time to finally be honest: but this time, because I want to.

"I've been so caught up trying to find the perfect man, but you're not perfect and I don't expect you to be." I take a deep breath and finally admit the truth. "Because I'm not perfect and I don't ever want to be."

I smile at my revelation as I wait for Oliver's reaction.

"Natalie, I never wanted you to be perfect—"

"I know you didn't, but I wanted to be perfect. I thought that it was my fault, something that I was doing wrong, and that's why I hadn't found love yet."

"Natalie, of course it's not your fault." Oliver frowns. "It was my fault."

"What?" Now I frown at his words. "Why would it possibly be your fault?"

"Because it took me so long to find you."

I slowly lean forward and press my lips to his with a desire so great. I draw back to look in his eyes, but Oliver grabs my face and presses his lips against mine again, more forcefully than before, and I get lost in his touch. He runs his fingers though my hair and I wrap my arms around him, holding on and hoping to never let go.

I feel Oliver smile against my lips and then put his forehead to mine.

An hour later, sitting on Oliver's lap as he gently strokes my arm I can't help but sigh as I remember I have work waiting for me on my desk. Oliver tries to convince me to stay and I'll be honest, his arguments are very enticing, but I promise to make it up to him later tonight.

"Though we probably shouldn't flaunt it at work. You know, show people how in love we are," I argue, though I'm secretly hoping he will object. I would love to flaunt our relationship to anyone who will listen. "I mean, if you are going to be working here for a while, we should try to be professional. Oh– maybe we could come up with some sort of secret code!"

Oliver laughs and shakes his head. "I plan to be around forever, remember?"

The smile on his face is contagious. "I was hoping you were going to say that."

The hungry look that enters his eyes makes me want to abandon my career and just stay in his arms for the rest of my life. With a final parting kiss, I get up and walk over to his office door, stepping over a box with files stuffed in it to reach for the handle.

"Natalie?" Oliver asks.

With my hand resting on the knob I turn and look at him.

"Yes?"

"I would love to take you to a *business meeting* tonight," Oliver gives an exaggerated wink.

I try and fight the amusement on my face, but the prospect of this code talk is too exciting. "I would love to go to a *business meeting* with you tonight."

Standing behind his desk once again, he lifts some files from on top of his computer and I still love the sight of his forearms flexing; in fact, I know I will never get tired of it.

"Great, there's this new sushi restaurant that just opened by my flat."

"Oh– er– sushi?" I ask.

I don't know what the huge deal with this sushi is. I'm not very good with uncooked things...

"Yes," Oliver nods then frowns. "Unless you would like something else?"

"No, sushi is great."

"You're sure?" Oliver looks at me as though he is not convinced.

I look over my shoulder as I open the door and smile.

"Would I lie?"

To The Man of My Dreams,

I've finally found you. The search is over.

I'll be seeing you soon,

Natalie Flemming.

P.S. Just in case Johnny Depp is reading this, please still feel free to contact me. I'm sure we could work something out.

ABOUT THE AUTHOR

Emily Harper has a passion for writing humorous romance stories where the heroine is not your typical damsel in distress. Throughout her novels you will find love, laughter, and the unexpected!

Originally from England, she currently lives in Canada with her wonderful husband, beautiful daughter, mischievous son, and a very naughty dog.

Made in the USA
Charleston, SC
11 December 2013